Edgar Wallace was born illegitimat
adopted by George Freeman, a porte
eleven, Wallace sold newspapers at L
school took a job with a printer. He enlisted in the Royal West Kent
Regiment, later transferring to the Medical Staff Corps and was sent
to South Africa. In 1898 he published a collection of poems called
The Mission that Failed, left the army and became a correspondent
for Reuters.

Wallace became the South African war correspondent for *The
Daily Mail*. His articles were later published as *Unofficial Dispatches* and
his outspokenness infuriated Kitchener, who banned him as a war
correspondent until the First World War. He edited the *Rand Daily
Mail*, but gambled disastrously on the South African Stock Market,
returning to England to report on crimes and hanging trials. He
became editor of *The Evening News*, then in 1905 founded the Tallis
Press, publishing *Smith*, a collection of soldier stories, and *Four Just
Men*. At various times he worked on *The Standard*, *The Star*, *The Week-
End Racing Supplement* and *The Story Journal*.

In 1917 he became a Special Constable at Lincoln's Inn and also
a special interrogator for the War Office. His first marriage to Ivy
Caldecott, daughter of a missionary, had ended in divorce and he
married his much younger secretary, Violet King.

The Daily Mail sent Wallace to investigate atrocities in the Belgian
Congo, a trip that provided material for his *Sanders of the River* books.
In 1923 he became Chairman of the Press Club and in 1931 stood as
a Liberal candidate at Blackpool. On being offered a scriptwriting
contract at RKO, Wallace went to Hollywood. He died in 1932, on
his way to work on the screenplay for *King Kong*.

BY THE SAME AUTHOR
ALL PUBLISHED BY HOUSE OF STRATUS

- The Admirable Carfew
- The Angel of Terror
- The Avenger (USA: The Hairy Arm)
- Barbara On Her Own
- Big Foot
- The Black Abbot
- Bones
- Bones In London
- Bones of the River
- The Clue of the New Pin
- The Clue of the Silver Key
- The Clue of the Twisted Candle
- The Coat of Arms (USA: The Arranways Mystery)
- The Council of Justice
- The Crimson Circle
- The Daffodil Mystery
- The Dark Eyes of London (USA: The Croakers)
- The Daughters of the Night
- A Debt Discharged
- The Devil Man
- The Duke In the Suburbs
- The Face In the Night
- The Feathered Serpent
- The Flying Squad
- The Forger (USA: The Clever One)
- The Four Just Men
- Four Square Jane
- The Fourth Plague
- The Frightened Lady
- Good Evans
- The Hand of Power
- The Iron Grip
- The Joker (USA: The Colossus)
- The Just Men of Cordova
- The Keepers of the King's Peace
- The Law of the Four Just Men
- The Lone House Mystery
- The Man Who Bought London
- The Man Who Knew
- The Man Who Was Nobody
- The Mind of Mr J G Reeder (USA: The Murder Book of J G Reeder)
- More Educated Evans
- Mr J G Reeder Returns (USA: Mr Reeder Returns)
- Mr Justice Maxell
- Red Aces
- Room 13
- Sanders
- Sanders of the River
- The Sinister Man
- The Square Emerald (USA: The Girl from Scotland Yard)
- The Three Just Men
- The Three Oak Mystery
- The Traitor's Gate
- When the Gangs Came to London

The Door with Seven Locks

Copyright © David William Shorey
as Executor of Mrs Margaret Penelope June Halcrow otherwise Penelope Wallace.

All rights reserved. No part of this publication may be reproduced, stored in a retrieval system, or transmitted, in any form, or by any means (electronic, mechanical, photocopying, recording, or otherwise), without the prior permission of the publisher. Any person who does any unauthorised act in relation to this publication may be liable to criminal prosecution and civil claims for damages.

The right of Edgar Wallace to be identified as the author of this work has been asserted..

This edition published in 2001 by House of Stratus, an imprint of Stratus Holdings plc, 24c Old Burlington Street, London, W1X 1RL, UK. Also at: Suite 210, 1270 Avenue of the Americas, New York, NY 10020, USA.

www.houseofstratus.com

Typeset, printed and bound by House of Stratus.

A catalogue record for this book is available from the British Library and the Library of Congress

ISBN 1-84232-677-5

This book is sold subject to the condition that it shall not be lent, resold, hired out, or otherwise circulated without the publisher's express prior consent in any form of binding, or cover, other than the original as herein published and without a similar condition being imposed on any subsequent purchaser, or bona fide possessor.

This is a fictional work and all characters are drawn from the author's imagination. Any resemblances or similarities to persons either living or dead are entirely coincidental.

We would like to thank the Edgar Wallace Society for all the support they have given House of Stratus. Enquiries on how to join the Edgar Wallace Society should be addressed to:
The Edgar Wallace Society, c/o Penny Wyrd, 84 Ridgefield Road, Oxford, OX4 3DA. Email: info@edgarwallace.org Web: http://www.edgarwallace.org/

TO MY FRIEND
H B LAWFORD, ESQ. ("A JUST MAN")

1

Dick Martin's last official job (as he believed) was to pull in Lew Pheeney, who was wanted in connection with the Helborough bank robbery. He found Lew in a little Soho café, just as he was finishing his coffee.

"What's the idea, colonel?" asked Lew, almost genially, as he got his hat.

"The inspector wants to talk to you about that Helborough job," said Dick.

Lew's nose wrinkled in contempt.

"Helborough grandmothers!" he said scornfully. "I'm out of that bank business – thought you knew it. What are you doing in the force, Martin? They told me that you'd run into money and had quit."

"I'm quitting. You're my last bit of business."

"Too bad you're falling down on the last lap!" grinned Lew. "I've got forty-five well-oiled alibis. I'm surprised at you, Martin! You know I don't 'blow' banks; locks are my speciality – "

"What were you doing at ten o'clock on Tuesday night?"

A broad smile illuminated the homely face of the burglar.

"If I told you, you'd think I was lying."

"Give me a chance," pleaded Dick, his blue eyes twinkling.

Lew did not reply at once. He seemed to be pondering the dangers to too great frankness. But when he had seen all sides of the matter, he spoke the truth.

"I was doing a private job – a job I don't want to talk about. It was dirty, but honest."

"And were you well paid?" asked his captor, polite but incredulous.

"I was – I got one hundred and fifty pounds on account. That makes you jump, but it is the truth. I was picking locks, certainly the toughest locks I've ever struck, and it was a kind of horrible job I wouldn't do again for a car-load of money. You don't believe me, but I can prove that I spent the night at the Royal Arms, Chichester, that I was there at eight o'clock to dinner and at eleven o'clock to sleep. So you can forget all that Helborough bank stuff. I know the gang that did it, and you know 'em too, and we don't change cards."

They kept Lew in the cells all night whilst inquiries were pursued. Remarkably enough, he had not only stayed at the Royal Arms at Chichester, but had stayed in his own name; and it was true that at a quarter to eleven, before the Helborough bank robbers had left the premises, he was taking a drink in his room, sixty miles away. So authority released Lew in the morning and Dick went into breakfast with him, because, between the professional thief-taker and the professional burglar, there is no real ill-feeling, and Sub-Inspector Richard Martin was almost as popular with the criminal classes as he was at police headquarters.

"No, Mr Martin, I'm not going to tell you anything more than I've already told you," said Lew good-humouredly. "And when you call me a liar, I'm not so much as hurt in my feelings. I got a hundred an' fifty pounds, and I'd have got a thousand if I'd pulled it off. You can guess all round it, but you'll never guess right."

Dick Martin was eyeing him keenly.

"You've got a good story in your mind – spill it," he said.

He waited suggestively, but Lew Pheeney shook his head.

"I'm not telling. The story would give away a man who's not a good fellow, and not one I admire; but I can't let my personal feelings get the better of me, and you'll have to go on guessing. And I'm not lying. I'll tell you how it happened."

He gulped down a cup of hot coffee and pushed cup and saucer away from him.

"I don't know this fellow who asked me to do the work – not personally. He's been in trouble for something or other, but that's no business of mine. One night he met me, introduced himself, and I went to his house – brr!" he shivered. "Martin, a crook is a pretty clean man – at least all the crooks I know; and thieving's just a game with two players; me and the police. If they snooker me, good luck to 'em! If I can beat them, good luck to me! But there's some dirt that makes me sick, just makes my stomach turn over. When he told me the job he wanted me for, I thought he was joking, and my first idea was to turn it in right away. But I'm just the most curious creature that ever lived, and it was a new experience, so, after a lot of thinking, I said 'Yes.' Mind you, there was nothing dishonest in it. All he wanted to do was to take a peep at something. What there was behind it I don't know. I don't want to talk about it, but the locks beat me."

"A lawyer's safe?" suggested the interested detective.

The other shook his head. He turned the subject abruptly; spoke of his plans – he was leaving for the United States, to join his brother, who was an honest builder.

"We're both going out of the game together, Martin," he smiled. "You're too good a man for a policeman, and I'm too much of a gentleman to be on the crook. I shouldn't be surprised if we met one of these days."

Dick went back to the Yard to make, as he thought, a final report to his immediate chief.

Captain Sneed sniffed.

"That Lew Pheeney couldn't fall straight," he said; "if you dropped him down a well, he'd wear away the brickwork. Honest robber! He's got that out of a book. You think you've finished work, I suppose?"

Dick nodded.

"Going to buy a country house and be a gentleman? Ride to hounds and take duchesses into dinner – what a hell of a life for a grown man!"

Dick Martin grinned at the sneer. He wanted very little persuasion to withdraw his resignation; already he was repenting – and, despite the attraction of authorship which beckoned ahead, he would have given a lot of money to recall the letter he had sent to the commissioner.

"It's a queer thing how money ruins a man," said Captain Sneed sadly. "Now if I had a six-figure legacy I should want to do nothing."

His assistant might sneer in turn.

"You want to do nothing, anyway," he said; "you're lazy, Sneed — the laziest man who ever filled a chair at Scotland Yard."

The fat man who literally filled and overflowed the padded office chair in which he half sat and half lay, a picture of inertia, raised his reproachful eyes to his companion.

"Insubordination," he murmured. "You're not out of the force till tomorrow — call me 'sir' and be respectful. I hate reminding you that you're a paltry sub-inspector and that I'm as near being a superintendent as makes no difference. It would sound snobbish. I'm not lazy, I'm lethargic. It's a sort of disease."

"You're fat because you're lazy, and you're lazy because you're fat," insisted the lean-faced young man. "It's a sort of vicious circle. Besides, you're rich enough to retire if you wanted."

Captain Sneed stroked his chin reflectively. He was a giant of a man, with the shoulders of an ox and the height of a Grenadier, but he was admittedly inert. He sighed heavily, and, groping in a desk basket, produced a blue paper.

"You're a common civilian tomorrow — but my slave today. Go along to Bellingham Library; there has been a complaint about stolen books."

Sub-Inspector Dick Martin groaned.

"It's not romantic, I admit," said his superior with a slow, broad smile; "kleptomania belongs to the dust and debris of detective work, but it is good for your soul. It will remind you, whilst you're loafing on the money you didn't earn, that there are a few thousand of your poor comrades wearin' their feet into ankles with fool inquiries like this!"

Dick (or "Slick" as he was called for certain reasons) wondered as he walked slowly down the long corridor whether he was glad or sorry that police work lay behind him and that on the morrow he might pass the most exalted official without saluting. He was a "larceny man", the cleverest taker of thieves the Yard had known.

Sneed often said that he had the mind of a thief, and meant this as a compliment. He certainly had the skill. There was a memorable night when, urged thereto by the highest police official in London, he had picked the pocket of a Secretary of State, taken his watch, his pocket-book, and his private papers, and not even the expert watchers saw him perform the fell deed.

Dick Martin came to the Yard from Canada, where his father had been governor of a prison. He was neither a good guardian of criminals nor youth. Dick had the run of the prison, and could take a stick pin from a man's cravat before he had mastered the mysteries of algebra. Peter du Bois, a lifer, taught him to open almost any kind of door with a bent hairpin; Lew Andrevski, a frequent visitor to Fort Stuart, made a specially small pack of cards out of the covers of the chapel prayer books, in order that the lad should be taught to conceal three cards in each tiny palm. If he had not been innately honest, the tuition might easily have ruined him.

"Dicky's all right – he can't know too much of that crook stuff," said the indolent Colonel Martin, when his horrified relatives expostulated at the corruption of the motherless boy. "The boys like him – he's going into the police and the education's worth a million!"

Straight of body, clear-eyed, immensely sane, Dick Martin came happily through a unique period of test to the office. The war brought him to England, a stripling with a record of good work behind him. Scotland Yard claimed him, and he had the distinction of being the only member of the Criminal Investigation Department who had been appointed without going through a probationary period of patrol work.

As he went down the stone stairs, he was overtaken by the third commissioner.

"Hello, Martin! You're leaving us tomorrow? Bad luck! It is a thousand pities you have money. We're losing a good man. What are you going to do?"

Dick smiled ruefully.

"I don't know – I'm beginning to think I've made a mistake in leaving at all."

The "old man" nodded.

"Do anything except lecture," he said, "and, for the Lord's sake, don't start a private agency! In America detective agencies do wonderful things – in England their work is restricted to thinking up evidence for divorces. A man asked me only today if I could recommend – "

He stopped suddenly at the foot of the stairs and viewed Dick with a new interest.

"By Jove! I wonder – ! Do you know Havelock, the lawyer?"

Dick shook his head.

"He's a pretty good man. His office is somewhere in Lincoln's Inn Fields. You'll find its exact position in the telephone directory. I met him at lunch and he asked me – "

He paused, examining the younger man with a speculative eye.

"You're the very man – it is curious I did not think of you. He asked me if I could find him a reliable private detective, and I told him that such things did not exist outside the pages of fiction."

"It doesn't exist as far as I'm concerned," smiled Dick. "The last thing in the world I want to do is to start a detective agency."

"And you're right, my boy," said the commissioner. "I could never respect you if you did. As a matter of fact, you're the very man for the job," he went on, a little inconsistently. "Will you go along and see Havelock, and tell him I sent you? I'd like you to help him if you could. Although he isn't a friend of mine, I know him and he's a very pleasant fellow."

"What is the job?" asked the young man, by no means enthralled at the prospect.

"I don't know," was the reply. "It may be one that you couldn't undertake. But I'd like you to see him – I half promised him that I would recommend somebody. I have an idea that it is in connection with a client of his who is giving him a little trouble. You would greatly oblige me, Martin, if you saw this gentleman."

The last thing in the world Dick Martin had in mind was the transference of his detective activities from Scotland Yard to the sphere of private agencies; but he had been something of a protégé of the third commissioner, and there was no reason in the world why he should not see the lawyer. He said as much.

"Good," said the commissioner. "I'll phone him this afternoon and tell him you'll come along and see him. You may be able to help him."

"I hope so, sir," said Dick mendaciously.

2

He pursued his leisurely way to the Bellingham Library, one of the institutions of London that is known only to a select few. No novel or volume of sparkling reminiscence has a place upon the shelves of this institution, founded a hundred years ago to provide scientists and *littérateurs* with an opportunity of consulting volumes which were unprocurable save at the British Museum. On the four floors which constituted the building, fat volumes of German philosophy, learned and, to the layman, unintelligible books on scientific phenomena, obscure treatises on almost every kind of uninteresting subject, stood shoulder to shoulder upon their sedate shelves.

John Bellingham, who in the eighteenth century had founded this exchange of learning, had provided in the trust deeds that "two intelligent females, preferably in indigent circumstances," should form part of the staff, and it was to one of these that Dick was conducted.

In a small, high-ceilinged room, redolent of old leather, a girl sat at a table, engaged in filing index cards.

"I am from Scotland Yard," Dick introduced himself. "I understand that some of your books have been stolen?"

He was looking at the packed shelves as he spoke, for he was not interested in females, intelligent or stupid, indigent or wealthy. The only thing he noticed about her was that she wore black and that her hair was a golden-brown and was brushed into a fringe over her forehead. In a vague way he supposed that most girls had hair of golden-brown, and he had a dim idea that fringes were popular among working-class ladies.

"Yes," she said quietly, "a book was stolen from this room whilst I was at luncheon. It was not very valuable – a German volume written by Haeckel called 'Generelle Morphologie.'"

She opened a drawer and took out an index card and laid it before him, and he read the words without being greatly enlightened.

"Who was here in your absence?" he asked.

"My assistant, a girl named Helder."

"Did any of your subscribers come into this room during that time?"

"Several," she replied. "I have their names, but most of them are above suspicion. The only visitor we had who is not a subscriber of the library was a gentleman named Stalletti, an Italian doctor, who called to make inquiries as to subscription."

"He gave his name?" asked Dick.

"No," said the girl to his surprise; "but Miss Helder recognized him; she had seen his portrait somewhere. I should have thought you would have remembered his name."

"Why on earth should I remember his name, my good girl?" asked Dick a little irritably.

"Why on earth shouldn't you, my good man?" she demanded coolly, and at that moment Dick Martin was aware of her, in the sense that she emerged from the background against which his life moved and became a personality.

Her eyes were grey and set wide apart; her nose straight and small; the mouth was a little wide – and she certainly had golden-brown hair.

"I beg your pardon!" he laughed. "As a matter of fact" – he had a trick of confidence which could be very deceptive – "I'm not at all interested in this infernal robbery. I'm leaving the police force tomorrow."

"There will be great joy amongst the criminal classes," she said politely, and when he saw the light of laughter in her eyes, his heart went out to her.

"You have a sense of humour," he smiled.

"You mean by that, that I've a sense of *your* humour," she answered quickly. "I have, or I should very much object to being called 'my good girl' even by an officer of the law" – she looked at his card again – "even with the rank of sub-inspector."

There was a chair at his hand. Dick drew it out and sat down unbidden.

"I abase myself for my rudeness, and humbly beg information on the subject of Signor Stalletti. The name means no more to me than John Smith – the favourite pseudonym of all gentlemen caught in the act of breaking through the pantry window in the middle of the night."

For a second she surveyed him gravely, her red lips pursed.

"And you're a detective?" she said, in a hushed voice. "One of those almost human beings who protect us while we sleep!"

He was helpless with laughter.

"I surrender!" He put up his hands. "And now, having put me in my place, which I admit is a pretty lowly one, perhaps you will pass across a little information about the purloined literature."

"I've no information to pass across." She leaned back in her chair, looking at him interestedly. "The book was here at two o'clock; it was not here at half-past two – there may be finger-prints on the shelf, but I doubt it, because we keep three charladies for the sole purpose of cleaning up finger-prints."

" But who is Stalletti?"

She nodded slowly.

"That was why I expressed a little wonder about your being a detective," she said. "My assistant tells me that he is known to the police. Would you like to see his book?"

"Has he written a book?" he asked in genuine surprise.

She got up, went out of the room and returned with a thin volume, plainly bound. He took the volume in his hand and read the title.

"New Thoughts on Constructive Biology, by Antonio Stalletti."

Turning the closely printed leaves, broken almost at every page by diagrams and statistical tables, he asked: "Why did he get into trouble with the police? I didn't know that it was a criminal offence to write a book."

"It is," she said emphatically; "but not invariably punished as such. I understand that the law took no exception to Mr Stalletti being an author; and that his offence was in connection with vivisection or something equally horrid."

"What is all this about?" He handed the book back to her.

"It is about human beings," she said solemnly, "like you and me; and how much better and happier they would be if, instead of being mollycoddled – I think that is the scientific term – they were allowed to run wild in a wood and fed on a generous diet of nuts."

"Oh, vegetarian stuff!" said Slick contemptuously.

"Not exactly vegetarian. But perhaps you would like to become a subscriber and read it for yourself?"

And then she dropped her tone of banter.

"The truth is, Mr – er – " – she looked at his card again – "Martin, we are really not worried about the loss of this book of Haeckel's. It is already replaced, and if the secretary hadn't been such a goop he wouldn't have reported the matter to the police. And I beg of you" – she raised a warning finger – "if you meet our secretary that you will not repeat my opinion of him. Now please tell me something that will make my flesh creep. I've never met a detective before; I may never meet one again."

Dick put down the book and rose to his seventy-two inches.

"Madam," he said, "I have not mustered courage to ask your name, I deserve all the roasting you have given me, but as you are strong, be merciful. Where does Stalletti live?"

She picked up the book and turned back the cover to a preface.

"Gallows Cottage. That sounds a little creepy doesn't it? It is in Sussex."

"I can read that for myself," he said, nettled, and she became instantly penitent.

"You see, we aren't used to these exciting interludes, and a police visitation gets into one's head. I really don't think the book's worth bothering about, but I suppose my word doesn't go very far."

"Was anybody here: besides Stalletti?"

She showed him a list of four names.

"Except Mr Stalletti, I don't think anybody is under suspicion. As a matter of fact, the other three people were severely historical, and biology wouldn't interest them in the slightest degree. It could not have happened if I had been here, because I'm naturally rather observant."

She stopped suddenly and looked at the desk. The book that had been lying there a few seconds before had disappeared.

"Did you take it?" she asked.

"Did you see me take it?" he challenged.

"I certainly didn't. I could have sworn it was there a second ago."

He took it from under his coat and handed it to her.

"I like observant people," he said.

"But how did you do it?" She was mystified. "I had my hand on the book and I only took my eyes off for a second."

"One of these days I'll come along and teach you," he said with portentous gravity, and was in the street before he remembered that, clever as he was, he had not succeeded in learning the name of this very capable young lady.

Sybil Lansdown walked to the window which commanded a view of the square and watched him till he was out of sight, a half-smile on her lips and the light of triumph in her eyes. Her first inclination was to dislike him intensely; she hated self-satisfied men. And yet he wasn't exactly that. She wondered if she would ever meet him again – there were so few amusing people in the world, and she felt that – she took up the card – Sub-Inspector Richard Martin might be very amusing indeed.

3

Dick was piqued to the extent of wishing to renew the encounter, and there was only one excuse for that. He went to the garage near his flat, took out his dingy Buick and drove down to Gallows Hill. It was not an easy quest, because Gallows Hill is not marked on the map and only had a local significance; and it was not until he was on the edge of Selford Manor that he learnt from a road-mender that the cottage was on the main road and that he had come about ten miles out of his way.

It was late in the afternoon when he drew abreast of the broken wall and hanging gate behind which was the habitation of Dr Stalletti. The weed-grown drive turned abruptly to reveal a mean-looking house, which he thought was glorified by the name of cottage. So many of his friends had "cottages" which were mansions, and "little places" which were very little indeed, when he had expected to find a more lordly dwelling.

There was no bell, and he knocked at the weather-stained door for five minutes before he had an answer. And then he heard a shuffling of feet on bare boards, the clang of a chain being removed, and the door opened a few inches.

Accustomed as he was to unusual spectacles, he gaped at the man who was revealed in the space between door and lintel. A long, yellow face, deeply lined and criss-crossed with innumerable lines till it looked like an ancient yellow apple; a black beard that half-covered its owner's waistcoat; a greasy skull-cap; a pair of black, malignant eyes blinking at him – these were his first impressions.

"Dr Stalletti?" he asked.

"That is my name." The voice was harsh, with just the suggestion of a foreign accent. "Did you wish to speak with me? Yes? That is extraordinary. I do not receive visitors."

He seemed in some hesitation as to what he should do, and then he turned his head and spoke to somebody over his shoulder, and in doing so revealed to the detective a young, rosy, and round-faced man, very newly and smartly dressed. At the sight of Dick the man stepped back quickly out of sight.

"Good-morning, Thomas," said Dick Martin politely. "This is an unexpected pleasure."

The bearded man growled something and opened the door wide.

Tommy Cawler was indeed a sight for sore eyes. Dick Martin had seen him in many circumstances, but never so beautifully and perfectly arrayed. His linen was speckless; his clothes were the product of a West End tailor.

"Good-morning, Mr Martin." Tommy was in no sense abashed. "I just happened to call round to see my old friend Stalletti."

Dick gazed at him admiringly.

"You simply ooze prosperity! What is the game now, Tommy?"

Tommy closed his eyes, a picture of patience and resignation.

"I've got a good job now, Mr Martin – straight as a die! No more trouble for me, thank you. Well, I'll be saying goodbye, doctor."

He shook hands a little too vigorously with the bearded man and stepped past him and down the steps.

"Wait a moment, Tommy. I'd like to have a few words with you. Can you spare me a moment whilst I see Dr Stalletti?"

The man hesitated, shot a furtive glance at the bearded figure in the doorway.

"All right," he said ungraciously. "But don't be long, I've got an engagement. Thank you for the medicine, doctor," he added loudly.

Dick was not deceived by so transparent a bluff.

He followed the doctor into the hall. Farther the strange man did not invite him.

"You are police, yes?" he said, when Dick produced his card. "How extraordinary and bizarre! To me the police have not come for a long time – such trouble for a man because he experiments for science on a leetle dog! Such a fuss and nonsense! Now you ask me – what?"

In a few words Dick explained his errand, and to his amazement the strange man answered immediately: "Yes, the book, I have it! It was on the shelf. I needed it, so I took it!"

"But, my good man," said the staggered detective, "you're not allowed to walk off with other people's property because you want it!"

"It is a library. It is for lending, is it not? I desired to borrow, so I took it with me. There was no concealment. I placed it under my arm, I lifted my hat to the young signora, and that was all. Now I have finished with it and it may go back. Haeckel is a fool; his conclusions are absurd, his theories extraordinary and bizarre." (Evidently this was a favourite phrase of his.) "To you they would seem very dull and commonplace, but to me – " He shrugged his shoulders and uttered a little cackle of sound which Dick gathered was intended to be laughter.

The detective delivered a little lecture on the systems of loaning libraries, and with the book under his arm went out to rejoin the waiting Mr Cawler. He had at least an excuse for returning to the library, he thought with satisfaction.

"Now, Cawler" – he began without superfluous preliminaries and his voice was peremptory – "I want to know something about you. Is Stalletti a friend of yours?"

"He's my doctor," said the man coolly.

He had a merry blue eye, and he was one of the few people who had passed through his hands for whom Dick had a genuine liking. Tommy Cawler had been a notorious "knocker-off" of motor-cars, and a "knocker-off" is one who, finding an unattended machine, steps blithely into the driver's seat and is gone before the owner misses his machine. Tommy's two convictions had both been due to the unremitting inquiries of the man who now questioned him.

"I've got a regular job; I'm chauffeur to Mr Bertram Cody," said Tom virtuously. "I'm that honest now, I wouldn't touch anything crook, not to save my life."

"Where does Mr Cody live when he's at home?" asked Dick, unconvinced.

"Weald House. It is only a mile from here; you can step over and ask if you like."

"Does he know about your – sad past?" Dick questioned delicately.

"He does; I told him everything. He says I am the best chauffeur he ever had."

Dick examined the man carefully.

"Is this the – er – uniform that your employer prefers?"

"I'm going on a holiday, to tell you the truth," said Mr Cawler. "The governor is pretty good about holidays. Here's the address if you want it."

He took an envelope from his pocket addressed to himself, "c/o Bertram Cody, Esq., Weald House, South Weald, Sussex."

"They treat me like a lord," he said, not without truth. "And a more perfect lady and gentleman than Mr and Mrs Cody you'd never hope to see."

"Fine," said the sceptical Richard. "Forgive these embarrassing questions, Tommy, but in my bright lexicon there is no such word as 'reform.'"

"I don't know your friend, but you've got it wrong," said Tommy hazily.

Martin offered him a lift, but this was declined, and the detective went back along to London, and, to his annoyance, arrived at the library half an hour after the girl had left.

It was too late, he thought, to see Mr Havelock of Lincoln's Inn Fields, and in point of fact the recollection of that engagement brought with it a feeling of discomfort. His plans were already made. He intended spending a month in Germany before he returned to the work which he had promised himself: a volume on "Thieves and Their Methods", which he thought would pleasantly occupy the next year.

Dick, without being extremely wealthy, was in a very comfortable position. Sneed had spoken of a six-figure legacy, and was nearly right, although the figures were dollars, for his uncle had been a successful cattle farmer of Alberta. Mainly he was leaving the police force because he was nearing promotion, and felt it unfair to stand in the way of other men who were more in the need of rank than himself. Police work amused him. It was his hobby and occupation, and he did not care to contemplate what life would be without that interest.

He had turned to go into his flat when he heard a voice hail him, and he turned to see the man whom he had released that morning crossing the road in some haste. Ordinarily, Lew Pheeney was the coolest of men, but now he was almost incoherent.

"Can I see you, Slick?" he asked, a quiver in his voice, which Dick did not remember having heard before.

"Surely you can see me. Why? Is anything wrong?"

"I don't know." The man looked up and down the street nervously. "I'm being trailed."

"Not by the police – that I can swear," said Dick.

"Police!" said the man impatiently. "Do you think that would worry me? No, it's the fellow – I spoke to you about. There's something wrong in that business. Slick, I kept one thing from you. While I was working I saw this guy slip a gun out of his hip and drop it into his overcoat pocket. He stood holding it all the time I was working, and it struck me then that, if I'd got that door open, there'd have been no chance of my ever touching the thousand. Halfway through I said I wanted to go out, and, once outside, I bolted. There was something that chased me – God knows what it was; a sort of animal. And I hadn't got a gun – I never carry one in this country, because a judge piles it on if you're caught with a barker in your pocket."

All the time they had been speaking they were passing through the vestibule and up the stairs to Slick's flat, and, without invitation, the burglar followed him into the apartment.

He led the man into his study and shut the door.

"Now, Lew, let me hear the truth – what was the work you were doing on Tuesday night?"

Lew looked round the room, out of the window, everywhere except at Dick. Then: "I was trying to open a dead man's tomb!" he said in a low voice.

4

There was a silence of a minute. Dick looked at the man, hardly believing his ears.

"Trying to open a dead man's tomb?" he repeated. "Now sit down and tell me all about it, Lew."

"I can't — yet. I'm scared," said the other doggedly. "This man is hell, and I'd as soon face the devil as go through another night like I had on Tuesday."

"Who is the man?"

"I won't tell you that," said the other sullenly. "I might at the end, but I won't tell you now. If I can find a quiet place I'm going to write it all out, and have it on paper in case — anything happens to me."

He was obviously labouring under a sense of unusual excitement, and Dick, who had known him for many years, both in England and in Canada, was amazed to see this usually phlegmatic man in such a condition of nerves.

He refused to take the dinner that the old housekeeper served, contenting himself with a whisky and soda, and Dick Martin thought it wise not to attempt to question him any further.

"Why don't you stay here tonight and write your story? I won't ask you for it, but you'll be as safe here as anywhere."

That idea seemed already to have occurred to the man, for he obeyed instantly, and Dick gathered that he had some such scheme in his mind. Dinner was nearly through when the detective was called away to the phone.

"Is that Mr Martin?"

The voice was that of a stranger.

"Yes," replied Dick.

"I am Mr Havelock. The commissioner sent me a message this evening, and I was expecting you to call at my office. I wonder if you could see me tonight?"

There was anxiety and urgency in the tone. "Why, surely," said Dick. "Where are you living?"

"907, Acacia Road, St John's Wood. I am very near to you; a taxi would get you here in five minutes. Have you dined? I was afraid you had. Will you come up to coffee in about a quarter of an hour?"

Dick Martin had agreed before he realized that his guest and his strange story had to be considered.

The startling announcement of Lew Pheeney had changed his plans. Yet it might be advisable to leave the man to write his story. He called his housekeeper aside and dismissed her for the night. Pheeney, alone in the flat, might write his story without interruption.

The man readily agreed to his suggestion, seemed, in fact, relieved at the prospect of being alone, and a quarter of an hour later Mr Martin was ringing the bell of an imposing house that stood in its acre of garden in the best part of St John's Wood. An elderly butler took his stick and hat and conducted him into a long dining-room, furnished with quiet taste. Evidently Mr Havelock was something of a connoisseur, for of the four pictures that hung on the wall, Dick accurately placed one as being by Corot, and the big portrait over the carved mantelpiece was undoubtedly a Rembrandt.

The lawyer was dining in solitary state at the end of a long, polished table. A glass of red wine stood at his elbow, a long, thin cigar was between his teeth. He was a man between fifty and sixty, tall and rather thin. He had the brow and jaw of a fighter, and his iron-grey side-whiskers gave him a certain ferocious appearance. Dick liked him, for the eyes behind his horn-rimmed spectacles were very attractive.

"Mr Martin, eh?" He half rose and offered his firm, thin hand. "Sit down. What will you drink? I have a port here that was laid down for princes. Walters, give Mr Martin a glass."

He leaned back in his chair, his lips pursed, and regarded the young man fixedly.

"So you're a detective, eh?" It sounded reminiscent of an experience he had had that morning, and Dick grinned. "The commissioner says you're leaving the police force tomorrow, and that you want a hobby. By heavens, I'll furnish you a hobby that'll save me a lot of sleepless nights! Walters, serve Mr Martin and clear out. And I am not to be interrupted. Switch off the phone; I'm not at home to anybody, however important."

When the door had closed behind the butler, Mr Havelock rose and began a restless pacing of the room. He had a quick, abrupt, almost offensively brusque manner, jerking out his sentences accusatively.

"I'm a lawyer – you probably know my name, though I've never been in a police court in my life. I'm very seldom in any court of law. I deal with companies and estates, and I'm trustee for half a dozen, or maybe a dozen, various charities. I'm the trustee of the Selford estate." He said this with a certain emphasis, as though he thought that Dick would understand the peculiar significance of this. "I'm the trustee of the Selford estate," he said again, "and I wish to heaven I wasn't. Old Lord Selford – not that he was old, except in sin and iniquity, but the late Lord Selford, let me say – left me sole executor of his property and guardian of his wretched child. The late Lord Selford was a very unpleasant, bad-tempered man, half mad, as most of the Selfords have been for generations. Do you know Selford Manor?"

Dick smiled.

"Curiously enough, I was on the edge of it today. I didn't know there was such a place until this afternoon, and I had no idea there was a Lord Selford – does he live there?"

"He doesn't." Havelock snapped the words, his eyes gleaming fiercely from behind his glasses. "I wish to God he did! He lives nowhere. That is to say, he lives nowhere longer than two or three days together. He is a nomad of nomads; his father in his youth was something of the same nature. Pierce – that is his family name, by the way, and he has always been called Pierce – has spent the last ten years wandering from town to town, from country to country, drawing heavily upon his revenue, as he can well afford to do because it is a large one, and returning to England only at the rarest intervals. I haven't seen him for four years." He said this slowly.

"I'll give you his history, Mr Martin, so that you will understand it better," he went on. "When Selford died, Pierce was six. He had no mother, and, curiously enough, no near relations. Selford was an only child, and his wife was also in that position, so that there were no uncles and aunts to whom I could have handed over my responsibility. The boy was delicate, as I found when I sent him to a preparatory school at the age of eight, expecting to be rid of the poor little beggar, but not a day passed that he didn't send me a note asking to be taken away. Eventually I found a private tutor for him, and he got some sort of education. It was not good enough to enable him to pass the Little Go – that is the entrance examination to Cambridge – and I sent him abroad with his tutor to travel. I wish to heaven I hadn't! For the travel bug bit deep into his soul, and he's been moving ever since. Four years ago he came to me in London. He was then on his way to America, where he was studying economic conditions. He had a wild idea of writing a book – one of the delusions from which most people suffer is that other people are interested in their recollections."

Dick flushed guiltily, but the lawyer went on, without apparently noticing his embarrassment.

"Now I'm worried about this boy. From time to time demands come through to me for money, and from time to time I cable him very respectable sums – which, of course, he is entitled to receive, for he is now twenty-four."

"His financial position – " began Dick.

"Perfectly sound, perfectly sound," said Mr Havelock impressively. "That isn't the question at all. What is worrying me is, the boy being so long out my sight. Anything may happen to him; he may have fallen into the worst possible hands." He hesitated, and added: "And I feel that I should get in touch with him – not directly, but through a third person. In other words, I want you to go to America next week, and, without saying that you came from me, or that I sent you, get acquainted with Lord Selford – he travels, by the way, as Mr John Pierce. He is a very quick mover, and you'll have to make careful inquiries as to where he has gone, because I cannot promise that I can keep you as well informed of his movements as I should like. If, in your absence, I have a cable from him, I will, of course, transmit it to you. I want you to find Pierce, but in no circumstances are you to acquaint the police of America that you are following him, or that there is anything suspicious in his movements. All that I want to know is, has he contracted any undesirable alliance, is he a free agent, is the money I send to him being employed for his own benefit? He tells me, by the way, that he has bought a number of shares in industrial concerns in various parts of the world, and some of these shares are in my possession. A great number, however, I cannot account for, and he has replied to my inquiries by telling me that they are safely deposited with a South African banking corporation. The reason I ask you to keep this matter entirely to yourself is because, you will understand, I can't have him embarrassed by the attentions of the local authorities. And most earnestly I am desirous that he should not know I sent you. Now, Mr Martin, how does the idea appeal to you?"

Dick smiled.

"It looks to me like a very pleasant sort of holiday. How long will this chase last?"

"I don't know – a few months, a few weeks: it all depends upon the report I receive from you, which, by the way, must be cabled to me direct. I have a very free hand and I can allow you the limit of expenses; in addition to which I will pay you a handsome fee."

He named a sum which was surprisingly munificent.

"When would you want me to go?"

The lawyer took out a little pocket-book and evidently consulted a calendar.

"Today is Wednesday; suppose you leave next Wednesday by the *Cunarder*? At present he is in Boston, but he tells me that he is going to New York, where he will be staying at the Commodore. Boston is a favourite hunting ground of his." His lips twitched. "I believe he intends sparing a chapter to the American War of Independence," he said dryly; "and, naturally, Boston will afford him an excellent centre for that study."

"One question," said Dick, as he rose to go. "Have you any reason to suppose that he has contracted, as you say, an undesirable alliance – in other words, has married somebody that he shouldn't have married?"

"No reason at all, except my suspicious mind," smiled Mr Havelock. "If you become friendly with him, as I am perfectly sure with an effort you could succeed in doing, there are certain things I would like you to urge upon him. The first of these is that he comes back to England and takes his seat in the House of Peers. That is very essential. Then I should like him to have a London season, because it's high time he was married and off my mind. Selford Manor is going to ruin for want of an occupant. It is disgraceful that a fine old house like that should be left to the charge of a caretaker – anyway, he ought to come back to be buried there," he added, with a certain grim humour, and Dick did not quite understand the point of this remark until eight months later.

The task was, in Dr Stalletti's words, extraordinary and bizarre, but it was not wholly unusual. Indeed, the first thought he had was its extreme simplicity. The commission was really a holiday on a grand scale, and something of his regret at leaving Scotland Yard was expunged by the pleasant prospect.

It was nine o'clock on this wet October night when he came into Acacia Road. There was not a cab in sight, and he had to walk half a mile before he reached a rank. Letting himself into his flat, he found it in darkness, and to his surprise Pheeney had gone. The remains of the dinner were on the table – he had told the housekeeper that he would clear the board, but one corner of the tablecloth had been turned up, and there were on the cleared space half a dozen sheets of paper and a fountain pen. Evidently Lew intended returning, but though Dick Martin waited up until two o'clock, there was no sign of the grave-robber. For some reason Pheeney had changed his mind.

At half-past ten the next morning he called at the library with his book. The girl looked up with a little laugh as he came in.

"I admit I'm a good joke," he said ruefully. "Here is your book. It was taken by an ignorant foreigner, who believed that loaning libraries are run on rather haphazard lines."

She stared at the book. "Really, you are most impressive, Mr Martin. Please tell me how you did it."

"Sheer deduction," he said gaily. "I knew the man who took it was a foreigner, because you told me so. I guessed his address because you gave it me; and I recovered the book by the intricate process of asking for it!"

"Wonderful!" she breathed, and they laughed together.

There was small excuse for his lingering, yet he contrived, as she hinted rather plainly, to hinder her for the greater part of an hour. Happily, the patrons of the Bellingham Library were not early risers, and she had the best part of the morning to herself.

"I am going abroad next week for a few months," he said carelessly. "I don't know why I tell you, but I thought possibly you would be interested in foreign travel."

She smiled to herself.

"You are certainly the naïvest detective I have ever met! In fact, the only detective I have ever met!" she added. Then, seeing his obvious discomfiture, she became almost kind. "You see, Mr Martin, I have been very well brought up" – even in her kindness, her irony made him wince – "which means that I am fearfully conventional. I wonder if you can guess how many men one meets in the course of a week who try to interest you in their family affairs? I'm not being unkind really," she smiled, as he protested.

"I've been rather a brute – I'm awfully sorry," said Dick frankly, "and I deserve all the roasting you give me. But it's very natural that even a humble detective officer should wish to improve an acquaintance with one who, if I may say so without bringing a blush to your maiden cheeks, has a singularly attractive mind."

"And now let us all be complimentary," she said, though the colour in her face was heightened and her eyes were a little brighter. "You are the world's best detective, and if ever I lose anything, I am sending immediately for you."

"Then you'll draw a blank," said Dick triumphantly. "I'm leaving the force and becoming a respectable member of society tomorrow, Miss — ?"

She did not attempt to help him.

Then suddenly he saw a look of understanding come to her face.

"You're not the man that Mr Havelock is sending to look for my relative, are you?"

"Your relative?" he asked in amazement. "Is Lord Selford a relative of yours?"

She nodded.

"He's a forty-second cousin, heaven knows how many times removed. Father was his second cousin. Mother and I were dining with Mr Havelock the other night, and he said that he was trying to get a man to run Selford to earth."

"Have you ever met him?" asked Dick.

She shook her head.

"No, but my mother knew him when he was a small boy. I think she saw him once. His father was a horror. I suppose Mr Havelock has told you that — I am assuming that my guess is right: you are going in search of him?"

Dick nodded.

"That was the sad news I was trying to break to you," he said.

At that moment their *tête-à-tête* was interrupted by the arrival of an elderly gentleman with a vinegary voice, who, Dick guessed, was the secretary.

He went back to Scotland Yard to find Captain Sneed, who had been absent when he had called on the phone that morning. Sneed listened without comment to the extraordinary story of Lew Pheeney's midnight occupation.

"It certainly sounds like a lie, and anything that sounds like a lie generally is a lie," he said. "Why didn't Pheeney stay, if he'd got this thing on his conscience? And who was chasing him? Did you see anybody?"

"Nobody," said Dick. "But the man was afraid, and genuinely so."

"Humph!" said Sneed, and pressed a bell.

To the clerk who answered: "Send a man to pick up Pheeney and bring him here. I want to ask him a few questions," he said. And then, calling the man back: "You know his address, Dick. Go along and see if you can unearth him."

"My term of service expires at twelve today."

"Midnight," said Sneed laconically. "Get busy!"

Lew Pheeney lived in Great Queen Street, at a lodging he had occupied for years; but his landlady could give no information. Pheeney had left the previous afternoon somewhere about five and had not returned. A haunt of the burglar was a small club, extensively patronized by the queer class which hovers eternally on the rim of the law. Pheeney had not been there – he usually came in to breakfast and to collect his letters.

Dick saw a man who said he had had an engagement with Pheeney on the previous night, and that he had waited until twelve.

"Where am I likely to find him?"

Here, however, no information was forthcoming. Dick Martin's profession was as well known as Mr Pheeney's.

He reported the result of his visits to Sneed, who for some reason took a more serious view of the whole matter than Dick had expected.

"I'm believing it now, that grave-robbing story," said Sneed, "and certainly it's remarkable if Lew was upset, because nothing short of an earthquake would raise a squeal with him. Maybe he's at your flat?"

When Dick got home the flat was empty. His housekeeper had neither seen nor heard from the visitor. The detective strolled into his bedroom, pulled off his coat, intending to put on the old shooting jacket he wore when he was writing – for he had a number of reports to finish before he made his final exit from the Yard.

The coat was not hanging up where it was usually kept, and he remembered that his housekeeper had told him that she had put it in the bureau: a tall piece of mahogany furniture where his four suits were invariably hung on hangers.

Without a thought he turned the handle of the bureau door and pulled it open. As he did so, the body of a man fell against him, almost knocking him over, and dropped to the floor with an inanimate thud. It was Lew Pheeney, and he was dead.

5

The Big Five at Scotland Yard filled Dick Martin's dining-room, waiting for the verdict of the medical man who had been hastily summoned. The doctor came in in a few minutes.

"So far as I can tell by a superficial examination," he said, "he's been dead for some hours, and was either strangled or else his neck was broken."

In spite of his self-control, Dick shivered. He had slept in the room that night, where, behind the polished door, lay that ghastly secret.

"There was no sign of a struggle, Martin?" asked one of the officers.

"None whatever," said Dick emphatically. "I am inclined to agree with the doctor: I should think that he was struck by something heavy and killed instantly. But how they got into the flat, God knows!"

Inquiries of the girl who worked the night elevator were unsatisfactory, because she could remember nobody having come into the flat after Dick had gone out.

The six detectives made a minute examination of the premises.

"There's only one way he could have come in," said Sneed when the inspection was over, "and that is through the kitchenette."

There was a door in the kitchen leading to a tiny balcony, by the side of which ran an outside service lift, used, as Dick explained, to convey tradesmen's parcels from the courtyard below, and worked from the ground level by a small handle and winch.

"You don't remember if this kitchen door was bolted?" asked Sneed.

The troubled young man explained that he had not been in the kitchen after his return on the previous night. But his housekeeper, who was hovering tearfully in the background, volunteered the information that the door was open when she had come that morning.

Dick looked down into the yard. The flat was sixty feet from the ground, and although it was possible that the intruder had climbed the ropes of the service lift, it seemed a feat beyond the power of most burglars.

"He gave you no indication as to who the man was he feared?" asked Sneed, when the rest of the Yard officers had gone back to headquarters.

"No," Dick shook his head. "He told me nothing. He was scared, and I'm sure his story was perfectly true – namely, that he was engaged to rob a grave, and that he had an idea that the man who made the engagement would have killed him if he had succeeded in his task."

Dick went down to Lincoln's Inn Fields that morning and had an interview with Mr Havelock, who had already read the account in the evening newspapers, though Lew's strange story was suppressed by the police even at the inquest.

"Yes, I was afraid this might interfere with our plans, but I'm not particular to a week or two, and if you must remain behind for inquiries, I will still further extend the period. Though in a sense the matter is urgent, it is not immediately so."

There was a conference of Yard officials, and it was agreed that Dick should be allowed to leave England immediately after the inquest, unless an arrest was made, on the understanding that he was to keep in touch with headquarters, so that, should the murderer be found, it would be possible for him to return to give evidence at the trial. This arrangement he conveyed to Mr Havelock.

The inquest was held on the Friday, and, after Dick's evidence, adjourned for an indefinite period. On the Saturday morning at twelve o'clock he left England, on the wildest chase that any man had ever undertaken. And behind him, did he but know it, stalked the shadow of death.

6

When Dick Martin left England on his curious quest, the Pheeney murder bulked largely in the newspapers, and almost as largely in his mind. There were other thoughts and other fancies to occupy the voyage, and, long after the memory of the murdered cracksman had faded, there remained with him the vision of two grey eyes that were laughing at him all the time, and the sound of a low, sweet, teasing voice.

If he had only had the sense to have discovered her name before he left. He might have written to her, or, at least, sent her picture post-cards of the strange lands through which he travelled. But, in the hurry of his departure, and occupied as he was with the Pheeney crime, though he played no official part in the inevitable inquiries which followed, he had neither the time nor the excuse to call upon her. A letter addressed to "the pretty lady with the grey eyes at the Bellingham Library" might conceivably reach her, if there were no other lady employed in the building who also was favoured with eyes of that hue. On the other hand (he argued this quite gravely, as though it were an intelligent proposition) she might conceivably be annoyed.

From Chicago he sent a letter to the secretary of the library, enclosing a subscription, though he had no more need of scientific volumes than of a menagerie of wild cats. But he hoped that he would see her name on the receipt – it was not until the letter was posted that he realized that by the time the receipt returned to Chicago he would be thousands of miles away, and cursed himself for his folly.

Naturally he heard nothing from Sneed, and was compelled to depend upon such stray English papers as came his way to discover how the Pheeney mystery had developed. Apparently the police had made no arrest, and the record of the crime had dwindled to small paragraphs in odd corners of the newspapers.

He came to Cape Town from Buenos Aires, to miss his man by a matter of days, and there had the first cheerful news he had received since his search began. It was a cable from Havelock asking him to return home at once, and with a joyful heart he boarded the *Castle* boat at the quay. On that day he made his second important discovery, the first having been made in Buenos Aires.

In all his travels he had not once come up with the will-o'-the-wisp lordling whom he had followed half round the world, and the zest of the chase had already departed from him. From Cape Town to Madeira was a thirteen-day voyage by the intermittent steamer on which he travelled, having missed the mail by four days. To a man with other interests than deck sports, the peculiar characteristics of passengers, and the daily sweepstake, those thirteen days represented the dullest period Dick Martin had ever endured. And then, when the ship stopped to coal, the miracle happened. Just before the steamer left, a launch came alongside; half a dozen passengers mounted the stairs, and for a moment Dick thought he was dreaming.

It was she! There was no mistaking her. He could have picked her out of a million. She did not see him, nor did he make himself known to her. For now that they were, so to speak, under one roof, and the opportunity that he dreamed of had presented itself in such an unexpected fashion, he was curiously shy, and avoided her until almost the last day of the voyage.

She was coolness itself when at last they met.

"Oh yes, I knew you were on board. I saw your name in the passenger list," she said, and he was so agitated that he did not even resent the amusement in her eyes.

"Why didn't you speak to me?" he asked brazenly, and again she smiled.

"I thought you were here – on business," she said maliciously. "My steward told me that you spent most of your evenings in the smoke-room, watching people play cards. I was wondering when you were coming into the library. You're a subscriber now, aren't you?"

"Yes," he said awkwardly; "I believe I am."

"I know because I signed your receipt," she said.

"Oh, then, you're – " He paused expectantly.

"I'm the person that signed the receipt." Not a muscle of her face moved.

And then: "What is your name?" he asked bluntly.

"My name is Lansdown – Sybil Lansdown."

"Of course, I remember!"

"You saw it on the receipt, of course?"

He nodded.

"It was returned to the library through the Dead Letter Office!" she went on ruthlessly.

"I never knew a human being who could make a man feel quite as big a fool as you," he protested, laughing. "I mean, as you make me feel," he corrected hastily.

And that ended the conversation until the evening. On the dark deck, side by side, they talked commonplaces, until –

"Start Light on the port bow, sir," said a muffled voice on the bridge deck above.

The two people leaning over the rail in the narrow deck space forrard saw a splash of light quiver for the fraction of a second on the rim of the dark sea and vanish again.

"That *is* a lighthouse, isn't it?"

Dick edged a little closer to the girl, sliding himself stealthily along the broad rail.

"Start Light," he explained. "I don't know why they call it 'Start' – 'Finish' would be a better word, I guess."

A silence, then: "You are not American, are you?"

"Canadian by habit, British by birth – mostly anything people want me to be. A kind of renegade."

He laughed softly in the darkness.

"I don't think that is a nice word. I wondered if I should meet you when I came aboard at Madeira. There are an awful queer lot of people on board this ship."

"Thank you for those kind words," said Dick gravely, and she protested. He went on: "There never was an ocean-going ship that wasn't full of queer people. I'll give you a hundred million if you can travel on a packet where some passenger doesn't say 'My, what a menagerie!' about the others. No, Miss Lansdown, you're not being trite. Life's trite anyway. The tritest thing you can do is to eat and sleep. Try living originally and see how quick you go dead. Here's another queer thing about ships — you never have the nerve to talk to the people you like till you're only a day from port. What they do with themselves the rest of the time, I've never found out. Five days from Madeira — and I never spoke to you till this afternoon. That's proof."

She drew a little farther from him and straightened herself.

"I think I'll go below now," she said. "It is rather late and we have to get up early — "

"What you're really thinking," said Dick, very gently, "is that in a second or so I'll be pawing your hand and saying wouldn't it be wonderful if we could sail on like this for ever under the stars and everything. I'm not. Beauty attracts me, I admit it. I know you're beautiful because I couldn't find anything odd about your face." He heard her laughing. "That's beauty in a sentence — something that isn't odd. If your nose was fat and your eyes little and squeeny and your complexion like one of those maps that show the density of population, I'd have admired you for your goodness of heart, but I shouldn't have raved you into the Cleopatra class. I'll bet she wasn't much to look at, if the truth was known."

"Are you going abroad again?" She turned the talk into a way that was less embarrassing, but regretted the necessity.

"No — I'm staying in London: in Clargate Gardens. I've got a pretty nice little flat; you can sit in the middle of any room and touch the walls without stretching. But it's big enough for a man without ambitions. When you get to my age — I'll be thirty on the fourteenth of September: you might like to send me flowers — you're content to settle down and watch the old world wag around. I'll be glad to get back. London takes a hold of you, and just when you're getting tired of it, up comes a fog like glue-gas and you can't find your way out."

She sighed.

"Our flat is smaller than yours. Madeira was heaven after Coram Street!"

"What number?" asked Dick brazenly.

"One of the many," she smiled. "And now I really must go. Goodnight."

He did not walk back with her to the companionway, but strolled to the ship's side, where he could watch the slim figure as it passed quickly along the deserted deck.

He wondered what had taken her to Madeira, for he guessed that she was not one of those fortunate people who, to escape the rigours of an English winter, could afford to follow the path of the vernal equinox. She was much more pretty than he had thought – beautiful in a pale, Oriental way – it was the slant of her grey eyes that suggested the East – not pale exactly – and yet not pink. Perhaps it was the geranium red of her lips that, by contrast, gave the illusion of pallor. Thin? He decided that she was not that. He thought of thin people in terms of brittleness – and she was supple and plastic.

Amazed to find himself analyzing her charm, he strolled along the deck and turned into the smoking-room. Although the hour was past eleven, the tables were occupied, and by the usual crowd. He walked to one in the corner and stood watching the play until, after many uneasy and resentful glances, the big man who, up till his arrival, had been the most jovial and the most successful player threw down his cards.

"Goin' to bed," he growled, gathered up his winnings and rose.

He stopped before Slick.

"You won a hundred from me last week," he said. "You pay that back before you leave this ship."

"Will you have it in notes or money?" asked Dick Martin politely. "Or maybe you'd prefer a cheque?"

The big man said nothing for a moment, then: "Come outside," he said.

Dick followed him to the dim lights of the promenade deck.

"See here, mister, I've been waitin' a chance to talk to you – I don't know you, though your face is kind of familiar. I've been working this line for ten years and I'll stand for a little competition, but not much. What I won't stand for is a cheap skate like you takin' me on and skinnin' me for a century with a stacked deck of cards. Get me?"

"In fact, what your soul kind of pines for is honour amongst card-sharps," said Dick. "Ever seen this?"

He took a metal badge from his pocket, and the big man gurgled apprehensively.

"I'm not entitled to wear that now, because I've left the Royal Canadian Police," said Dick Martin, replacing the badge. "I carry it around for old times' sake. You remember me? I'd say you did! I pinched you in Montreal eight winters ago for selling mining stock that was unattached to any mine."

"Dick Martin – " The big man invoked a great personage.

In the seclusion of his cabin, which he shared with two of his confederates, the big fellow wiped the perspiration from his forehead and grew biographical.

"He's the feller that went up to the Klondyke and took Harvey Wells. He had a moustache then; that's why I didn't recognize him. That feller's mustard! His father was governor of the gaol at Fort Stuart and used to allow his kid to play around with the boys. They say he can do anything with a pack of cards except make it sing. He caught Joe Haldy by pickin' his pocket for the evidence, and Joe's as wide as Broad Street."

Next morning, Mr Martin came down the gangway plank of the *Grail Castle* carrying a suitcase in each hand. One of the Flack gang that attends all debarkations to look over likely suckers, marked his youth and jauntiness and hooked his friend, the steward, who was usually a mine of information.

"Mr Richard Martin; he's a reg'lar time chaser – came to the Cape from the Argentine; got to the Argentine from Peru an' China – been down to New Zealand and India – God knows where."

"Got any stuff?"

The steward was dubious.

"Must have – no, he's not a drummer – he had the best cabin on the ship and tipped well. Some boys came aboard at Cape Town and tried to catch him at bridge, but he beat 'em."

The prospecting member of the Flack crowd sneered.

"Card people scare suckers," he said, with all the contempt which a land thief has for his seagoing brother. "Besides, these Cape boats are too small, and everybody knows everybody else. A card man would starve on that line. So long, Harry."

Harry, the steward, returned the farewell indifferently and watched the tout hurry down to the examining shed. Martin was waiting for the arrival of the Customs officer with a bored expression on his lean brown face.

"Mr Martin, isn't it?" The advance guard of the confidence men smiled pleasantly as he offered his hand. "I'm Bursen – met you at the Cape," said the newcomer, keeping the high note of heartiness. "Awfully glad to see you again."

His hand was not taken. Two solemn blue eyes surveyed him thoughtfully. The tout was well dressed; his linen was expensive, the massive gold cigarette-case that peeped from his waistcoat pocket was impressive.

"We must. meet in town – "

"At Wandsworth Gaol – or maybe Pentonville," said Dick Martin deliberately. "Get to blazes out of this, you amateur tale-teller!"

The man's jaw dropped.

"Go back to your papa" – Dick's long forefinger dug the man's waistcoat, keeping time with his words – "or to the maiden aunt who taught you that line of talk, and tell him or her that suckers are fetching famine prices at Southampton."

"See here, my friend – " The shoreman began a bluster to cover his inevitable retreat.

"If I kick you into the dock, they'll hold me for the inquest – seep!"

The "con" man seeped. He was a little angry, a little scared, and very hot under the collar, but he kept well away from the brown-faced man until he saw the first train pull out.

"If he's not a copper, I'm a Dutchman," he said, and felt for his cigarette-case and the solace of shredded Virginia. The case was gone!

Precisely at that moment Mr Martin was extracting a cigarette from its well-filled interior, and, weighing the gold in his hand, had concluded that it was at least 15 carat and worth money.

"What a beautiful case!"

The girl sitting opposite to him stretched out her hand, a friendly assurance that was very pleasing to Dick Martin. In her simple tailored costume and a close-fitting little hat she was another kind of girl, radiating a new charm and a new fragrance.

"Yes, it's rather cute," Dick answered soberly. "I got it from a friend. Glad your holiday is over?"

She stifled a sigh as she gave the case back to him.

"Yes, in a way. It wasn't exactly a holiday, and it was dreadfully expensive. I can't speak Portuguese either, and that made it difficult."

He raised his eyebrows at that.

"But all the hotel folk speak English," he said, and she smiled ruefully.

"I wasn't one of the hotel folk. I lived in a little boarding-house on the Mount, and unfortunately the people I had to see spoke only Portuguese. There was a girl at the boarding-house who knew the language a little, and she was helpful. I might have stayed at home for all the good I did."

He chuckled.

"We're in the same boat. I've been thirty thousand miles rustling shadows!"

She smiled whimsically.

"Were you looking for a key, too?" she asked, and he stared at her.

"A which?"

She opened the patent leather bag that rested on her knees and took out a small cardboard box. Removing the lid, she shook into her hand a flat key of remarkable shape. It was rather like an overgrown Yale, except that the serrations were not confined to one edge, but were repeated in complicated ridges and protuberances on the other.

"That's certainly a queer-looking object," he said. "Was that what you were looking for?"

She nodded.

"Yes – though I didn't know this was all I should get from my trip. Which sounds a little mad, doesn't it? Only – there was a Portuguese gardener named Silva who knew my father. He used to be in the service of a relative of ours. Didn't I boast once that I was related to Lord Selford – by the way, what is he like?"

"Like the letter O, only dimmer," he said. "I never saw him."

She asked a question and then went on: "About three months ago a letter came to my mother. It was written in very bad English by a priest, and said that Silva was dead, and that before he died he asked her forgiveness for all the harm he had done to us. He left something which was only to be given into the hand of a member of our family. That sounds remarkable, doesn't it?"

Dick nodded, impatient for her to continue.

"Of course, it was out of the question for mother or I to go – we have very little money to spare for sea trips. But the day after we got the letter, we had another, posted in London and containing a hundred pounds in notes and a return ticket to Madeira."

"Sent by?"

She shook her head.

"I don't know. At any rate, I went. The old priest was very glad to see me; he told me that his little house had been burgled three times in one month, and that he was sure the burglars were after the little package he was keeping for me. I expected something very valuable, especially as I learnt that Senhor Silva was a very rich man. You can imagine how I felt when I opened the box and found – this key."

Dick turned the key over in his hand.

"Silva was rich – a gardener, you said? Must have made a lot of money, eh? Did he leave a letter?"

She shook her head.

"Nothing. I was disappointed and rather amused. For some reason or other, I put the key into the pocket of the coat I was wearing, and that was lucky or unlucky for me. I had hardly left the priest's house before a man came out of a side alley, snatched my bag, and was out of sight before I could call for help. There was nothing very valuable in the bag, but it was all very alarming. When I got on board ship, I put the key in an envelope and gave it to the purser."

"Nobody bothered you on the ship?"

She laughed quietly as at a good joke.

"Not unless you would call the experience of finding your trunk turned out and your bed thrown on to the floor a 'bother'. That happened twice between Madeira and Southampton. Is it sufficiently romantic?"

"It certainly is!" said Dick, drawing a long breath. He looked at the key again. "What number Coram Street?" he asked.

She told him before she realized the impertinence of the question.

"What do you think is the meaning of these queer happenings?" she asked as he passed the cardboard box back to her.

"It's surely queer. Maybe somebody wanted that key badly."

It seemed to her a very lame explanation.

She was still wondering what had made her so communicative to a comparative stranger when the train ran into Waterloo Station. She felt a little nettled by his casual farewell; a nod and he had disappeared behind the screen of other passengers and their friends who crowded the platform.

It was a quarter of an hour later before she retrieved her baggage from the welter of trunks that littered the vicinity of the baggage van. A porter found her a cab, and she was tipping him, when a man brushed past her, jostling her arm, whilst a second man bumped into her from the opposite side. Her bag slipped from her hand and fell to the pavement. Before she could stoop, a third man had snatched it from the ground, and, quick as lightning, passed it to an unobtrusive little man who stood behind him. The thief turned to fly, but a hand grasped his collar and jerked him round, and as his hands came up in defence, a fist as hard as ebony caught him under the jaw and sent him flying.

"Get on your feet, thief, and produce your bag-snatching permit!" said Dick Martin sternly.

7

At ten o'clock the next morning Dick Martin walked blithely into Lincoln's Inn Fields. The birds were twittering in the high trees, the square lay bathed in pale April sunshine, and as for Slick, he was at peace with the world, though he had travelled nigh on thirty thousand miles and had failure to report at the end of them.

Messrs Havelock and Havelock occupied an old Queen Anne house that stood shoulder to shoulder with other mansions of the period. A succession of brass plates on the door announced this as the registered office of a dozen corporations, for Mr Havelock was a company lawyer, who, though he never appeared in the courts, gave the inestimable benefit of his advice to innumerable and prosperous corporations.

Evidently the detective was expected, for the clerk in the outer office was almost genial.

"I will tell Mr Havelock you're here," he said, and came back in a few seconds to beckon the wanderer into the private sanctum of the senior partner.

As Dick Martin came in, he was finishing the dictation of a letter, and he smiled a welcome and nodded to a chair. When the dictation was done and the homely stenographer dismissed, he got up from the big writing-table, filling his pipe.

"So you didn't see him?" he asked.

"No, sir. I moved fast, but he was quicker. I got into Rio the day he left. I was in Cape Town just three days after he had gone on overland to Beira – and then I had your cable."

Havelock nodded solemnly, puffing at his pipe.

"The erratic devil!" he said. "You might have come up with him at Beira. He's there yet."

Walking to his desk he pressed a bell, and his secretary made a reappearance.

"Give me the Selford file – the current one," he said, and waited until she had returned and given him a large blue folder. From this he took a cable form and handed it to his visitor. Slick read:

"Havelock London. Who is this man Martin chasing after me? Have already mailed power of attorney. Please leave me alone. Shall be in London August.

PIERCE."

The cable was dated Cape Town three days before Dick had arrived there.

"I could hardly do anything else," said Mr Havelock, rubbing his nose irritably with his knuckle. "Did you hear anything about him?"

Dick chuckled.

"That fellow didn't stand still long enough for anyone to notice him," he said. "I've talked to hotel porters and reception clerks in seven kinds of broken English, and none of 'em had anything on him. He was in Cape Town the day the new High Commissioner arrived from England."

"Well," asked Havelock after a pause, "what has that to do with it?"

"Nothing." Another pause, and then: "What do you really suspect?" asked Dick.

Mr Havelock pursed his lips.

"I don't know," he admitted frankly. "At the worst that he has married, or has become entangled in some way with a lady whom he is not anxious to bring to England."

Dick fingered his chin thoughtfully.

"Have you had much correspondence from him?" And, when the other nodded: "May I see it?"

He took the portfolio from Mr Havelock's hand and turned the leaves. There were cablegrams addressed from various parts of the world, long and short letters, brief instructions, obviously in reply to some query that Havelock had sent.

"Those only take you back for a year. I have one or two cases filled with his letters, if you would like to see them?"

Dick shook his head.

"These are all in his handwriting?"

"Undoubtedly. There is no question that he is being impersonated, if that is what you mean."

The detective handed back the portfolio with a little grimace.

"I wish I'd caught up with him," he said. "I'd like to see what kind of bird he is, though I know a dozen young fellows whose feet start itching the moment they sit still. I'm sorry I haven't been more successful, Mr Havelock, but, as I say, this lad is a swift mover. Maybe at some later time I'll ask to see the whole of these letters; I'd like to study them."

"You can see them now if you wish," said the lawyer, reaching for the bell.

The detective stopped him.

"So far as the alliance is concerned, I think you can rest your mind. He was alone in New York and alone in San Francisco. He landed without any encumbrances at Shanghai, and I trailed him through India without there being a hint of a lady in the case. When he comes back in August I'd like to meet him."

"You shall." Mr Havelock smiled grimly. "If I can nail him down long enough to give you time to get here."

Dick went home, turning over in his mind two important problems, in his pocket a very handsome cheque for his services. The elderly woman who kept house for him was out marketing when he arrived. Sitting down at his desk, his head in his hands, his untidy hair rumpled outrageously, he went over the last six exciting months of his life, and at the end the question in his mind was not answered. Presently he pulled the telephone towards him and called Havelock.

"I forgot to ask you, why does he call himself Pierce?"

"Who? Oh, you mean Selford? That is his name. Pierce, John Pierce. I forgot to explain to you that he hated his title. Oh, did I? Have you an idea?"

"None," said Slick untruthfully, for he had several ideas.

He had unpacked all but one suitcase, and this he now proceeded to turn on to the table. It was full of documents, hotel bills, notes he had made in the course of his tour; and at the bottom of the case a square sheet of blotting-paper, which he took out carefully and held up to the light. It was the blotted impression left by an envelope: "Mr Bertram Cody, Weald House, South Weald, Sussex." There was no need to refresh his memory, for he had made a very careful note of the name and address. He had found that sheet of blotting-paper in the private sitting-room at the Plaza Hotel in Buenos Aires which had been occupied, forty-eight hours before his arrival, by the restless Mr Pierce. Nobody had used the room after he had gone until Dick had asked the hotel manager to show him the suite which his quarry had occupied.

He locked away the blotting-paper in a drawer of his desk, strolled into his bedroom, and stood for a long time looking at himself in the glass.

"Call yourself a detective, eh?" he demanded of his reflection, as his lips curled. "You poor, four-flushing mutt!"

He spent the remainder of the day learning a new card trick that he had picked up on the voyage over; an intricate piece of work, consisting of palming a card from the top of the pack and passing it so that it became the ninth card of the pack. With a stop-watch before him he practised, until he managed to accomplish the transfer in the fifteenth part of a second. Then he was satisfied. When dusk descended on the world, he got out his car and drove southward leisurely.

8

"Show him in," said Mr Bertram Cody.

He was a little bald man with a gentle voice and the habit of redundancy. He required five minutes to say all that any other man could express in three sentences. Of this fault, if fault it was, he was well aware and made a jest of his weakness.

Fixing his large gold-rimmed spectacles, he peered at the card again —

MR JOHN RENDLE,
194, COLLINS STREET, MELBOURNE.

The name meant nothing to Mr Cody. He had known a Rendle in the eighties, a highly respectable tea importer, but the acquaintance was so slight a one that it was hardly likely.

He had been studying a small pocket notebook when the visitor was announced; a red morocco case that had, in addition to diary and writing space, a little pocket for cards, slips for stamps, and a tiny flat purse. He pushed the book under a heap of papers at his hand as the stranger entered.

"Mr Rendle," said a woman's harsh voice in the shadowy part of the room where the door was, and there came out of the gloom a tall, good-looking young man who certainly bore no resemblance to the long-forgotten China merchant.

"Will you sit down?" said Mr Cody gently. "And will you please forgive the semi-darkness in which I live? I find that my eyes are not as good as they were, and the glare of lights produces a very painful effect. This table-lamp, carefully shaded as it is, supplies my needs adequately, though it is insufficient for my visitors. Fortunately, if you will forgive what may appear to you as a rudeness, I receive most of my callers in the daytime."

The visitor had a quick smile, and was evidently a man to whom the semi-darkness of the big, richly furnished library was in no sense depressing. He groped in the shadows for the chair, which revealed itself by the light on its polished back, and sat down.

"I'm sorry to come at this hour, Mr Cody, but I only arrived yesterday by the *Moldavia*."

"From China," murmured Mr Cody.

"From Australia – I transhipped at Colombo."

"The *Moldavia* did not call at Colombo owing to an outbreak of cholera," interrupted Mr Cody, more gently still.

The visitor laughed.

"On the contrary, it called, and I and some thirty passengers embarked. The outbreak was reported after we left port. You are confusing the *Moldavia* with the *Morania*, which missed the call a week later."

The colour deepened on Mr Cody's plump face. He was deeply wounded, and in his most tender part, for he had been guilty of an error of fact.

"I beg your pardon," he said in a hushed and humble voice. "I am humiliated to discover that I have made a mistake. It *was* the *Morania* – I beg your pardon! The *Moldavia* had a smooth voyage?"

"No, sir. We ran into the simoon and had three boats carried away – "

"The two lifeboats on the spar deck and a cutter on the aft deck," nodded Mr Cody. "You also lost a lascar – washed overboard. Forgive me for interrupting you, I am an omnivorous reader."

There was a pause in the conversation here. Mr Cody, his head on one side, waited expectantly.

"Now, perhaps – ?" he suggested, almost timidly.

Again the visitor smiled.

"I've called on a curious errand," he said. "I have a small farm near Ten Mile Station – a property which adjoins a station of yours in that part of the world."

Mr Cody nodded slowly. He had many properties in the overseas States: they were profitable investments.

"I have reason to believe that there is gold on your property," Rendle went on. "And I take this view because I am by training an engineer and I know something about metallurgy. Six months ago I made a discovery which, very naturally, I was not anxious to advertise until I was certain of my facts."

He talked lucidly of conglomerate and outcrop, and Bertram Cody listened, nodding his head from time to time. In the course of his description Mr Rendle unfolded a map on the desk – a small scale map that did not interest Bertram Cody at all.

"My theory is that there is a reef running from here to here – "

When his guest had reached the end of his discourse: "Yes – I know there is gold at Ten Mile Station: the discovery was made by our agent and duly reported to us, so that the fear you had, Mr – er – um – Rendle, that he was keeping his – er – find a secret, has no foundation. There is gold – yes. But not in paying quantities. The matter has already been reported in the newspaper press – um – you would not have seen that, of course. Nevertheless, I am grateful to you. Human nature is indeed a frail quality, and I cannot sufficiently thank you for your thoughtfulness and – um – the trouble to which you have been put."

"I understand that you bought this property from Lord Selford," asserted Mr Rendle.

The bald man blinked quickly, like a man who was dazzled by a bright light.

"From his – er – agents: an eminent firm of lawyers. I forget their names for the moment. His lordship is abroad, you know. I believe that he is difficult to get at." He spread out his plump hands in a gesture of helplessness. "It is difficult! This young man prefers to spend his life in travel. His agents hear of him in Africa – they have a letter from the – um – wild pampas of the Argentine – they send him money to

China – an adventurous life, my dear young friend, but unnerving to his – um – relations, if he has relations. I am not sure."

He shook his head and sighed; then, with a start, as though he were for the first time aware that there was an audience to his perturbations, he rose and held out both his hands.

"Thank you for coming," he breathed, and Mr Rendle found his own hand encased in two warm, soft palms. "Thank you for your interest. Life is a brighter place for such disinterestedness."

"Do you ever hear from him?" asked the visitor.

"From – um – his lordship? No, no! He is ignorant of my existence. Oh, dear, no!" He took the visitor's arm and walked with him to the door. "You have a car?" He was almost grateful to his guest for the possession of such an article. "I am glad. It looks like being a stormy night – and it is late. Half-past ten, is it not? A safe journey to town!"

He stood under the portico until the rear lights of the car had disappeared behind a clump of rhododendrons that bordered the drive, then he went back into the hall.

The stout, hard woman in black silk, who Dick had thought was Mr Cody's housekeeper, followed her husband into the study and closed the door behind him.

"Who was he?" she asked. Her voice was uneducated, strident, and complaining.

Mr Cody resumed his place behind the heavy writing-table and smiled blissfully as he lowered himself into the padded chair.

"His name is Dick Martin," he said, "and he is a detective."

Mrs Cody changed colour.

"Good Gawd! Detective! Bertie, what did he come here for?"

She was agitated; the fat, beringed hand that went up to her mouth was trembling.

"You're sure?" she quavered.

Mr Cody nodded.

"A clever man – but I expected him. I have at least three photographs of him. I wonder," said Mr Cody softly. "I really wonder!"

He slipped his hand under the heap of papers to find the little notebook, and suddenly his face went pale.

"It's gone – my book and the key – my God! the key!"

He reeled to his feet like a drunken man, blank terror in his face.

"It was when he showed me that map!" he muttered hoarsely. "I'd forgotten that the fellow is an expert thief. Shut that damned door. I want to telephone!"

9

Dick drove a six-cylinder coupé whose bodywork had seen better days, though he claimed for its engines that the world had not seen their equal. With his screen-wiper wiping furiously, he came cautiously along the Portsmouth Road, his big head-lamps staring whitely ahead. The rain was pelting down, and since he must have a window open, and that window was on the weather side, one arm and part of the shoulder of his rainproof coat were soon black and shining.

"107, Coram Street," said his subconscious mind; and he wondered why he had connected this satisfactory visit of his to Mr Bertram Cody with that trim girl who was so seldom absent from his thoughts.

From time to time his hand sought his pocket and the flat leather book that reposed at the bottom. There was something hard inside that purse; he thought it was money at first; and then, in a flash, he realized that it was the touch of this notebook which recalled Sybil Lansdown. He pulled the car up so quickly that it skidded across the road and only missed a ditch by a matter of inches. Straightening the machine, he switched on the interior light and examined his "find". Before he unfastened the thin flap of the purse, he knew what it contained. But he was unprepared for the shape and size of the key that lay in his palm. It was an almost exact replica, in point of size, of that which Sybil Lansdown had shown him in the train, and which was now in the strong-room of his bank.

Dick whistled softly to himself, replaced the book in his pocket, but slipped the key under the rubber mat beneath his feet. The enterprising gentlemen who had made such strenuous efforts, and gone to such expense, to secure Sybil Lansdown's key would not hesitate to hold up a car.

Dick was beginning to have a respect for the brethren of the keys, and had found for himself an adventure which surpassed in interest the chasing of peregrinating noblemen. He turned off the interior light and sent his car forward along the rain-swept road, meditating upon the weird character of his discovery. Cody had denied he was in communication with this strange Lord Selford – why? And what was the meaning of the key? Dick had seen the oily man push the book under the papers as he entered, and, out of sheer devilment and his love for discovery, had seized the first opportunity of extracting the case. He would compare the two keys in the morning.

In the meantime it would be well for him to keep his mind concentrated upon the road ahead. Once a lumbering lorry had almost driven him into the ditch, and now, with twenty miles to go, he saw ahead of him three red lights, and slowed his engine till he came within a dozen yards of them. They were red lamps, placed in a line on the road, and if they meant anything it was that the road was under repair and closed. And yet – he had passed the lorry going at full speed only a mile away. That must have come along the forbidden stretch of road.

He peered through the open window and saw on his right a dilapidated wall, the top of which was hidden under a blanket of wild ivy. He saw, by the lights of the head-lamps, a gap, where there was evidently a gate. All this he took in at a glance, and he turned to the scrutiny of the road and the three red lamps.

"Yes, yes," said Slick to himself, switched out all the lights of the car, and, taking something from his hip pocket, he opened the door quietly and stepped into the rain, standing for a while listening.

There was no sound, except the swish and patter of the storm. Keeping to the centre of the road, he advanced slowly towards the red lamps, picked up the middle of these and looked at it. It was very old; the red had been hastily painted on to the glass. The second lamp was more new, but of an entirely different pattern, and here also the glass pane had been covered by some red, transparent paint. And this was the case with the third lamp.

He threw the middle light into the ditch, and found a satisfaction in hearing the crash of glass. Then he came back to his car, got inside, slammed the door, and put his foot on the starter. The little motor whined round, but the engines did not move. There must be some reason for this, he thought, for the car was hot, and never before had it failed. Again he tried, without success; then, getting down from the machine, he walked to the back to examine the petrol tank. There was no need, for the little indicator dial said "Empty".

"Yes, yes," said Slick again, staring down at this evidence of his embarrassment.

He had filled up before he reached Mr Cody's house, but, be that as it may, here was a trustworthy indicator pointing starkly to "E", and when he tapped the tank it gave forth a hollow sound in confirmation.

He sniffed: the place reeked. Flashing his pocket-lamp on the ground, he saw a metal cap and picked it up, and then understood what had happened. The wet roadway was streaked opalescently. Somebody had taken out the cap and emptied his tank whilst he was examining the lights.

He refastened the cap, which was both airproof, waterproof, and foolproof, and which could only have been turned by the aid of a spanner; and he had heard no chink of metal against metal. He carried no reserve, so that he was stranded beyond hope of succour, unless –

He sent his lamp in the direction of the gateway. One of the hinges of the gate was broken, and the rotting structure leaned drunkenly against a laurel bush. Until then he had not dreamed that he was anywhere near Gallows Cottage. But now he recognized the place.

Keeping his light on, he went up the long avenue quickly. On either side was a tangle of thick bush, which had grown at its will, unattended by a gardener. Overhead the tall poplars met in an arch. Keeping the light glowing from side to side, he passed up the gloomy avenue. Suddenly he stopped. Under the shadow of the hedge he saw a long, narrow hole. It had been recently dug and was, he judged, six feet deep.

"That looks like a home from home," he shuddered, and passed on to the square, ugly house, which had once been covered by plaster, broken now in a dozen places, showing the bare brick beneath.

Never had it seemed so mean looking as when the broad beam of his lamp picked out the patches and fissures in its walls. The entrance was a high, narrow doorway, above which was a little wooden canopy, supported by two iron bars let into the brickwork – he noted these most carefully now. There was no sign of life; no dog barked. The place was dead – rotting.

He waited a second before he mounted the two steps that brought the knocker within reach. As the clapper fell, he heard the sound echoing hollowly through the hall. Had he been a stranger he might easily have imagined that the place was empty, he thought, when no reply came. He knocked again. In a few minutes he heard a sound of feet in the hall, the rusty crackle of a key being turned, and the jingling of chains. The door opened a foot, and there appeared in the light of Dick's lamp the long, sallow face and the black beard.

The apparition was so startling that Dick, expectant as he was, nearly dropped his lamp.

"Who is this? What is this?" asked a voice pettishly. "Petrol? You have lost your petrol? Ach! that is foolish. Yes, I can give you some, if you pay for it. I cannot afford to give anything away."

He gave no sign of recognition, but opened the door wider, and Dick walked into the hall, turning as he did so to face the man who had let him in. Dr Stalletti wore a black overall, belted at the waist, and indescribably stained. On his feet were a pair of long, Russian boots, worn and cracked and amateurishly patched. He had no collar. What Dick noticed first was that this strange person had not apparently washed since they last met. His big, powerful hands were grimy, his nails were almost like talons. By the light of the small oil-lamp he carried, Martin saw that the hall was expensively furnished; the carpet was thick and almost new, the hangings of velvet, the chairs and settees of gilt and damask, must have cost a lot of money. A silver chandelier hung from the plastered ceiling, and the dozen or so electric candles it held supplied a brilliant light to the room. But here, as in the passage, everything was inches thick in dust. It rose in a small cloud as he walked across the thick carpet.

"You wait here, please. I will get you petrol – one shilling and tenpence a gallon."

Dick waited, heard the feet of his host sound hollowly, and presently grow faint. He made a careful inspection of the room. There was nothing here to indicate either the character or the calling of this strange, uncleanly man.

Presently he heard the man returning and the thud of two petrol tins as they were put down in the hall, and then his strange benefactor appeared, dusting his hands.

"Four gallons of petrol of the highest grade."

The visitor might have been a stranger for all the signs he made of recognition, and yet Dick was sure that the man knew him; and as though he guessed his visitor's thoughts, the bearded man announced, with a certain amount of pomposity: "I am the Professor Stalletti. We have, I think, met. It was because of a book you came."

"That is so, professor." Dick was alert, somewhere inside him a warning voice was speaking insistently.

"You have heard of me – yes? It is known in science. Come, come, my friend, pay your money and be gone."

"I am much obliged to you, professor," drawled Dick. "Here's ten shillings – we won't quarrel about the change."

To his surprise, the bearded man pocketed the note with a smirk of satisfaction. Evidently he was not too proud to make a profit on the transaction.

Walking to the front door, he opened it, and Dick followed him, making his exit sideways and keeping his face to this queer-looking man. The professor opened his mouth as though he were going to speak, but changed his mind and slammed the door in his visitor's face, and as he did so, there came, from somewhere in the house, behind those blind windows, such a scream of fear and agony as made the detective's blood run cold. It was a wail that rose to a shriek and died sobbingly to silence.

Perspiration stood on Dick Martin's face, and for a second he had the mind to force his way back into the house and demand an explanation. And then he saw the senselessness of that move, and, carrying a petrol tin in either hand, made his way down the drive. He was wearing rubber-soled shoes that caused little or no noise, and he was glad, for now his ears must serve where his eyes failed. By reason of his burden he had to dispense with the use of his lamp.

He had passed that section of the hedge where he had seen the hole, when his quick ears detected something moving behind him. It was the faintest sound, and only one with his keen sense of hearing could have detected it above the noise of the falling rain. It was not a rustle; it was something impossible to describe. Dick turned round and began to walk backwards, staring into the pitch black darkness before him. The noise grew more distinct. A twig snapped in the bushes to his right. And then suddenly he saw his danger and dropped the tins. Before he could reach his gun he was at grips with a something, naked, hairless, bestial.

Huge bare arms were encircling his shoulders; a great hand was groping for his face, and he struck blindly at a bare torso, so muscled that, even as he struck, he realized that he was wasting his strength. Suddenly, with a mighty effort, he jerked round, gripped the huge arm with both his hands, and, stooping, jerked his assailant over his head. There was a thud, a groan, a ghastly sobbing, blubbering sound that was not human, and in the next fraction of a second Dick's automatic was in his hand and the safety catch pushed down.

"Stay where you are, my friend," he breathed. "I'd like to have a look at you."

He picked up the torch he had dropped and turned the light on the ground. Nobody was there. He flashed the lamp left and right without discovering a trace of his assailant. Was he behind him? Turning, he sent the rays in the direction of the house, and in that second caught sight of a great figure, naked except for a loin-cloth, disappearing into the bushes.

"Jumping snakes!" breathed Dick Martin, and lost not a second in reaching the road, refilled the empty tank, and started the engine.

In a little while he was following the road to London, absorbed in the problem of Dr Stalletti, and the big hole in the ground, recently dug, and intended, he did not doubt, for the reception of his own body.

10

Mr Cody was not a good walker, and was, moreover, a particularly fearful man; otherwise he might have walked the six miles which separated him from Gallows Cottage on a dark and windy night. Instead, he ordered his car, his chauffeur protesting sourly, and drove to within a hundred yards of the house.

"Back into that lane, put your lights out, and don't move until I return."

Mr Tom Cawler growled something under his breath.

"And don't you be long!" he said. "What is the game, anyway, Cody? Why didn't you get him to come over?"

"Mind your own dam' business!" snapped the little man, and disappeared into the darkness.

He reached the cottage soon after one o'clock, and groped his way up the dark drive. Once, as he put out his stick to feel his way, it almost dropped from under him. If he had been leaning his weight upon it he would have fallen into the pit which had been dug by the side of the path.

He did not knock at the door, but, making a half circuit of the house, tapped at one of the dark windows, and returned to find the front door open and Stalletti waiting in the hall.

"Ah, it is you! So strange to find you at such an hour! Come in, my very dear friend. I received your telephone message, but, alas! fate was against me."

"He got away?" asked the other fearfully.

Dr Stalletti shrugged and stroked his long beard.

"It was fate," he said. "Otherwise, he would be – quite close to us. I spread the lamps on the road, and myself emptied his petrol, and got back to the house before he came. The situation was extraordinary and remarkable. There was nothing between him and death but the thin end of this card." He held a soiled and greasy playing-card in his hand. He had been playing patience when the knock came. "There was one weak link, and so it snapped."

Cody looked round the gloomy hall like a man frightened.

"What will happen now?" he asked in a whisper.

Again the doctor shrugged.

"The police will come sooner or later, and they will make a search of my house. Does it matter? What shall they find here but a few rats lawfully dead?"

"Did you –?" Cody did not complete the question.

"I sent somebody after him, but somebody failed like a bungling idiot. You cannot develop muscle except at the expense of brain, my dear fellow. Will you come in?"

He led the way back to his workroom. The desk at which he worked had been cleared of its unpleasant properties, and was half covered with playing-cards.

"First you may tell me who is this man? I have seen him before. He came to me to ask some questions about a book. It was the day your chauffeur was here. I seem to know him, and yet I do not know him."

Cody licked his dry lips; his heavy face was white and drawn.

"He is the man Havelock sent after Selford," he muttered, and the doctor's eyebrows went up to a point.

"Can that possibly be? How extraordinary and bizarre! So he is the gentleman that the clever lawyer sent to look for Selford!"

He began to laugh, and the sound of his laughter was like the crackling of parchment.

"That is too good a joke! The real good, simple Havelock! So clever a man! And," he demanded archly, "did our friend find my lord? No? That is remarkable. Perhaps he did not move quick enough! Perhaps he went by train when airplanes were procurable!"

He seated himself at the table, tapping a tattoo with his uncleanly fingers upon its surface.

"What else does my friend want?" he asked, eyeing the other keenly.

"I want some money," said Cody, in a sulky voice.

Without a word, the doctor stooped down and unlocked a drawer of his desk, took out a battered tin cash-box, opened it, and extracted a thick bundle of notes.

"There are fewer to pay now," he said. "Therefore your money is increased. If I die, it will be to your benefit. *Per contra* – "

"Don't let us talk about death," shivered the little man, his trembling hands straying to his bald head. "We don't want any of that sort of thing; we've gone right away from our first idea, which was good. If you take life – "

"Have I taken life?"

"Have you?" demanded Cody, and waited.

The doctor's red mouth curled in a smile.

"There was a Mr Pheeney," he said carefully. "Is that how you name him? He certainly died, but I think that must have been suicide."

He chuckled again.

"I do not love people who go to policemen. That is very bad for business, because the police have no imagination. Now, suppose I go to a policeman" – he was eyeing the other from under his drooping lids – "and suppose I make statements – what a catastrophe!"

The little man jumped to his feet, quivering. "You dare not!" he said hoarsely. "You dare not!"

Again Stalletti shrugged his thin shoulders.

"Why do I stay in this cold and horrible country," he asked, "when I could be sitting on the *patio* of my own beautiful villa in Florence? There I would be away from these stupid policemen."

He stopped suddenly and raised his finger to signal for silence. Cody had not caught the faint squeak against the shuttered window, but the doctor had heard it twice.

"There is somebody outside," he whispered.

"Is it – ?"

Stalletti shook his head.

"No, it is not Beppo." His lips curled at the word, as though he were enjoying the best jest in the world. "Wait."

He crossed the room noiselessly and disappeared into the dingy passage. Cody heard the sound of a door being softly unlocked, and there was a long wait before the man returned. He was blinking as though the return to the light was painful to his eyes, but Cody had seen him in this condition before, and knew that this strange, unearthly man was labouring under an unusual emotion.

He carried in his hand a thing that looked like a telephone earpiece with a rubber attachment.

"Somebody was listening at the window, my friend. I will give you three guesses – you were not driven here by car?"

"I walked," said the other shortly.

"Your excellent chauffeur – he suffers from curiosity?"

"I tell you I walked. No chauffeur came with me."

"He could walk also. What is this?"

He took from his pocket a cap and laid it on the table.

"Do you recognize this – no?"

Cody shook his head.

"He had taken this off to put on the earpieces. The microphone I could not find. But he listened – yes."

"Who was it? It couldn't have been Cawler," said Cody fretfully. "He is my wife's nephew."

"And adores her?" sneered the doctor.

He turned the cap inside out, and read the name of the seller.

"How strange it would be if, after all, you harboured in your house a spy."

"How can that be?" said the other violently. "You know as much as I know about Cawler."

"And you know – what? Nothing except that he is a thief, a stealer of motor-cars, on whom the police have their eye all the time. When this friend of yours came, this Martini – Martin, is it? – he knew your Cawler, and I was instantly compromised."

Then Cody began to speak in a low, earnest tone, and the bearded man listened, at first with contemptuous indifference and then with interest.

"It is a pity that my Beppo was not in the grounds. We should have known for sure," he said at last.

Mr Cody walked half a mile along the road to where he had left his car. The chauffeur was dozing in his seat, but woke at the sound of his employer's voice.

"Cawler, have you been by the car all the time? Did you follow me?"

"Would I walk if I could ride?" growled the man. "Of course I've been here all the time. Why? Somebody been shadowing you?"

"You play the fool with me, my friend, and you'll be sorry."

"I'm never sorry for anything I've done," said the other coolly. "Get inside – it's raining."

He swung the car out of the main road and drove back to Weald House at breakneck speed. Amongst the many things which Mr Cody dreaded was fast driving, and the only way his chauffeur could get even at times was to do one of the things that the little man did not like. He got out, livid with rage, and spluttered an expletive at the unmoved chauffeur.

"You're giving yourself airs because you think you're indispensable, you – !"

Even while he was talking, the car moved on to its garage. As a debater, Tommy Cawler did not regard his master as being worthy of his metle.

11

Mr Havelock had scarcely reached his office the following morning when Dick arrived. The bushy brows of that gentleman rose at the sight of his visitor.

"I've come to make a confession, Mr Havelock," he began.

"That sounds ominous," said the other, his eyes twinkling.

"Maybe it's more ominous than it sounds," said Dick. "I've kept something back from you – information which ought to be in your hands."

Briefly he told the story of the blotting-paper he had found in the hotel at Buenos Aires.

"Obviously Lord Selford is in communication with this person. Because I wasn't quite sure how the land lay, and whether there was something behind Selford's absence from England, I took the trouble to investigate."

"Mr Bertram Cody?" frowned Havelock. "I seem to remember that name."

"Possibly you recall the sale of an Australian property – "

Havelock's face lightened.

"Why, of course, that is it!" he said. "There was some talk of gold being found on the property. I saw the announcement in *The Times*. Cody, of course! But he doesn't know Lord Selford."

"Then why should Selford write to him?"

"Perhaps he wrote to his lordship first," suggested Mr Havelock, obviously perturbed. "Did you ask him, by the way, whether he knew our young friend?"

Dick nodded.

"He denies all knowledge and all correspondence, which sounded queer to me. Have you ever seen anything like this?"

He laid on the table the little pocket-book he had taken from the doctor's desk, and, unfolding it, showed the key. Mr Havelock picked it up and examined it curiously.

"That is a queer-looking thing. What is it – a key?" he asked. "How did you get this?"

"I found it," said the unabashed Dick. "It was in a notebook that I – borrowed. You will see that the book is full of entries relating to Lord Selford's movements. Here is Buenos Aires and the date he was there; here is the date of his arrival in Shanghai; the date he left San Francisco – in fact, this is a very complete memorandum of Lord Selford's movements during the past eight months."

Havelock turned the pages slowly.

"This is certainly extraordinary," he said. "You say he denies knowing Selford?"

"Absolutely. He swore he'd never seen him or had any correspondence with him. Selford has done all his business in connection with the sale of the Australian property through you."

Mr Havelock nodded.

"That is true," he said. "I remember the circumstances well. My managing clerk carried through that transaction."

"Do you know a fellow named Stalletti? He lives in a house on the London road, halfway to Brighton."

He saw Mr Havelock start.

"Yes, I know Stalletti, but I haven't seen his house for years. As a matter of fact, it is one of Selford's properties, too – most of the land thereabouts is part of the Selford estate. Cody must be a leaseholder of ours. As for Gallows Cottage, I remember that we leased it to Stalletti after his trouble in London. He was prosecuted for practising vivisection without a licence," he explained. "An uncleanly, Svengali-looking man."

"That describes him so completely," said Dick, "that a policeman could recognize him!"

"What has he been doing?"

"Why, I'll tell you," said Dick slowly.

He had good reason for his tardiness, for the solution of the Selford mystery had come to him with dramatic suddenness, and he was trying to think of two things at one and the same time, to piece together loose ends to which he might well devote the labour of months. Nevertheless, his story was a fairly faithful narrative of his adventure.

"Have you been to the police?" asked Havelock, when he had finished.

"No, sir. I can never get it out of my mind that I am the police – all the police I'm interested in."

He scratched his chin meditatively.

"I certainly might have seen old man Sneed," he said.

"Who is Sneed?" demanded Havelock.

"A Scotland Yard man," replied Dick slowly. "Sneed's strong for mysteries."

"A detective?" he asked.

"Yes. What does Stalletti do for a living, Mr Havelock?"

"I'm blessed if I know," said the lawyer. "He is really a brilliant pathologist, but his experiments are a little too peculiar for the modern school. By Jove! I remember now. When Stalletti took the house, it was on the recommendation of Cody. Wait a moment, I'll turn it up."

He hurried from the room and came back in a few minutes with a letter-book in his hand.

"That is so," he said. "Cody, if you remember, had just bought the Australian property, and it was a month after that transaction was completed that we gave Stalletti a lease on Gallows Cottage. A dramatic name, Mr Martin, but a gallows in fact used to stand somewhere about there in the bad old times."

"It'll stand somewhere about there in the good new times," said Dick, " if that thug digs any more holes for me!"

He had learned all he wanted to know – indeed, much more than he expected; and he returned to Clargate Gardens only to pack his two suitcases and to give the astonished old woman who looked after the flat in his absence a month's holiday.

"I guess a month will be just long enough. You can go to the sea or you can go to the mountains, Rebecca. But there's one place that's barred, and it's this little old home of mine."

"But why, sir – ?" began the woman.

Dick was very firm on the point, uttered horrific threats as to what would happen to the lady if she dared so much as look in during the period of her leave.

His flat was one of many in an apartment block, and to the janitor he gave instructions about his letters, which were to be sent to Scotland Yard to await his arrival. He did not notify Mr Havelock of his plans, considering that at this stage of the special investigations which he was preparing to undertake, it would be advisable not to take any man into his confidence.

12

Mrs Lansdown and her daughter were people who lived as naturally in three rooms as they would have lived in a town house with twenty. A frail woman of remarkable beauty, Sybil's mother had had both experiences. There was a time of affluence when Gregory Lansdown had his thousand acres in Berkshire, a shoot in Norfolk, and a salmon river in Scotland, to say nothing of his handsome little house in Chelsea. But those possessions, with his racing stable, his steam yacht and the yearly trip to Algeria, had gone in a night. He was a director of a company that went into liquidation, following the hurried departure of a managing director who went eventually into prison. The directors were called upon to make good the best part of a million and a half, and Gregory Lansdown was the only one of them whose property was in his own name. He paid to the last farthing and died before his last payment was completed.

The Lansdowns retained one asset – the house in which they were now living, and which had been divided up into three self-contained flats before the blow fell. Into one of these, the smallest, Mrs Lansdown carried such of her personal belongings as she could salvage from the wreck of fortune.

They were sitting together on the night after Sybil's return, the mother reading, Sybil writing at the little escritoire in the corner of the sitting-room. Presently Mrs Lansdown put down her book.

"The trip was foolish – it was stupid of me to sanction it. I am worried a little about the consequence, dear. It is all so frantically unreal and fantastic that if it were anybody but you who had told me I should dismiss the story as a piece of romantic imagination."

"Who was Silva, mother?"

"The Portuguese? He was quite a poor man; a landscape gardener. Your father discovered him in Madeira and brought him to the notice of his cousin. I have always known that he was grateful to your dear father, who helped him in many ways. He became head gardener to our cousin – who was not the nicest man to work for; he had an unpleasant habit of thrashing servants who displeased him, and I believe he once struck Silva. Do you remember him, Sybil?"

Sybil nodded.

"A big, red-faced man with a tremendous voice – he used to drive in a carriage drawn by four horses. I hated him!"

Mrs Lansdown took up her book again, read a line or two, and then put it down.

"What is this man, Sybil?"

Sybil laughed.

"Mother, that is the fourth time you've asked me! I don't know. He was very nice and had wonderful blue eyes."

"A gentleman?"

"Yes," quickly. "Not a perfectly mannered man, I should think; very alert, very capable, a most trustable man."

Mrs Lansdown turned a page of her book without reading.

"What is he – his profession, I mean?"

Sybil hesitated.

"I don't know – now. He used to be a detective-inspector, but he has left the police force. Didn't I tell you?" And then, a little defiantly: "What is the social position of a detective?"

Her mother smiled to herself.

"About the same as a librarian, my dear," she said quietly. "In the matter of professions he is on the same plane as my little girl. It wasn't wise to ask you that."

The girl got up from the table, and, putting her arms about the elder woman, hugged her.

"You are thinking because I poured out my young heart to him, as they say in sentimental stories, that I'm in love with him. Well, I'm not! He amuses me awfully – he says the quaintest things. And I like him in spite of the strong language I heard him use to a man on the quay when I was waiting to get my baggage examined. He's very straight and clean. I feel that. I'm glad the wretched key was lost – I could have swooned on his neck for joy when he hit that horrible thief. But I'm no more in love with him than – He's probably married and has a large and rosy family."

There was a knock at the door. Sybil went to open it and gazed, open-eyed and in some embarrassment, at the subject of their conversation.

"Won't you come in, Mr Martin?" she said, a little awkwardly.

He walked past her into the tiny square hall, and presently followed her into the sitting-room. One shrewd glance the older woman gave him, and was satisfied.

"You're Mr Martin?" she smiled, as she took his hand in hers. "I wanted to thank you personally for your care of my daughter."

"I'm rather glad you mentioned that, because I didn't know exactly how I was going to start my interesting conversation," said Dick, choosing, to the girl's consternation, the least stable and most fragile of all the chairs in the room. "Safety first is a mighty well-hackneyed expression, but, like all these old slogans you're tired of hearing, it is concentrated truth. Your key, by the way, Miss Lansdown, is in my bank, and if anybody pushes you very hard you can tell them so."

She stared at him open-mouthed.

"But I thought the key was lost?"

"The bag was lost," he corrected. "When I handed you back that box on the train, I took the liberty of extracting the key; you heard it rattle, and it was heavy enough for a key, for I put a half-crown piece in the box."

"But it was never out of my sight!" gasped the girl.

Dick smiled sweetly.

"The art of ringing changes is to keep everything in sight."

"But it is impossible," said Sybil.

He had an exasperating habit of passing to the next subject without apology.

"Miss Lansdown, I'm going to shock you pretty badly. You had an idea, when you met me, that I was a respectable member of society. I was – I'm not today. I'm the nearest approach to a private detective you have ever met – and private detectives are nearly mean. You don't change colour, so I guess you're too numb to feel."

"My daughter had an idea you were in that profession," said Mrs Lansdown, her eyes dancing with amusement. She was beginning to understand the attraction this drawling man had for her daughter.

"I'm glad," said Dick soberly. "Now, when I start in to ask questions, you won't be thinking that I'm consumed with idle curiosity. You told me about your cousin," he said, addressing Sybil; "I'm anxious to know what other cousins Lord Selford has."

"None," said the girl. "Mother and I are his only living relatives – unless he is married."

She saw the change that came instantly to his face. The eyes narrowed, the mouth grew harder; something of his levity fell away from him.

"I was afraid of that," he said quietly. "I guessed it, and I was afraid of it. I knew that you were in this scheme somewhere, but I couldn't quite see how. Have you any friends in the country, ma'am?" he asked Mrs Lansdown.

"Yes, I have several," she answered in surprise. "Why?"

"You're on the telephone, are you not?" He glanced at the instrument that stood on the top of the escritoire. "Will you be prepared, at a minute's notice, to leave London? My first inclination was to ask you to leave tonight, but I don't think that will be necessary."

Mrs Lansdown eyed him steadily.

"Will you please tell me what this is all about?" she asked quietly.

He shook his head.

"I can't tell you now. I'm sort of coming out of a mist, and I'm not sure of the objects that are looming up. I honestly believe you are both safe from danger, and that nobody is going to give you any trouble – yet a while."

"Is all this about the key?" asked Sybil, listening in amazement.

"It is all about the key," he repeated, and she had never seen him so grave. "What sort of a man was the late Lord Selford?" He directed his question to the mother, and she made a little grimace.

"He was not a nice man," she said. "He drank, and there were one or two unsavoury incidents in his past that one doesn't like to talk about, even if one knew the true facts. But then, all the Selfords were a little queer. The founder of the house behaved so badly in the fifteenth century that he was excommunicated by the Pope. You have heard of the Selford tombs?"

He shook his head. To all appearances the words had no significance to him. Tombs! His mind flashed back to Lew Pheeney – the man who had died because he had seen too much – the robber of graves. He had to set his teeth and school the muscles of his face to impassivity.

"You are probably not interested in English antiquities," Mrs Lansdown was saying, "but if you are, I can give you some particulars. Strangely enough, I was reading them only this afternoon."

She got up and went to a bookshelf which stood in one corner, and took out a volume the vellum cover of which was yellow with age.

"This is one of the few treasures I possess," she said. "It is the original 'Baxter's Chronicle', printed in 1584, one of the first books that came from the Caxton Press."

She turned the stiff leaves and presently stopped.

"Here is the passage. You need not read about the offence which Sir Hugh committed – it is hardly creditable to our family."

He took the book and read where her finger pointed.

"Sir Hugh being under banne of church for hys synnes, and beinge denyed burialle such as is ryte for Christianne knyghtes, caused there to be dugge in the earthe a great burialle playce for hymme and ye sonnes of hys housse, the wyche ws calld the Sellfords Toomes, and this sayme ws blessd in proper fashion by Fr Marcus, a holy manne of ye time, butte in secrette because of ye sayed banne. And theyse toomes to the number of a score he caused to be made yn stonne curiously cutte wyth mannie angyles and saynts, wych ws wonderfull to see."

"For hundreds of years," said Mrs Lansdown, "the burial ground of the Selfords was unconsecrated, though that has been remedied since 1720."

"Where is the place?" asked the fascinated Dick.

"It is in a corner of Selford Park; a strange, eerie spot on the top of a small hill, and surrounded by old trees. They call it the Birdless Copse, because birds are never seen there, but I think that is because there is no open water for many miles."

He had to frame every word he spoke lest he betrayed the wild sense of exaltation he felt.

"Who is occupying the Manor House? I suppose there is a manor house attached to the park?"

She nodded.

"It is in the hands of a caretaker during Lord Selford's absence. Mr Havelock told me that our kinsman hates the place, and would sell it but for the fact that it is entailed."

He covered his face with his hand, trying to concentrate his thoughts.

"Have you ever seen this wandering Selford?"

"Only once, when he was a boy, whilst he was at school. He has written to me; in fact, I had a letter quite recently. I will get you the letter, if it would interest you? Are you very much interested in Lord Selford?"

"Very much," he said emphatically.

She went out of the room and came back with a small wooden box, which she opened. She sorted out a number of letters and presently placed one before him. It was from Berlin, and had been written in April of 1914:

"Dear Aunt,
"It is so many years since I have written to you, or you have heard from me, that I am almost ashamed to write. But knowing how interested you are in queer china, I am sending you by registered post an old German beer mug of the fifteenth century.
                              "Yours affectionately,
                                   "PIERCE."

The handwriting was the same as he had seen in Mr Havelock's office.

"Of course, I'm not his aunt," said Mrs Lansdown, still searching amongst the letters. "I am in reality his cousin twice removed. Here is another letter."

This, Dick saw, was sent from an hotel in Colombo, and was only a year old:

"I am making great progress with my book, though it is rather absurd to call a collection of disjointed notes (as it is at present) by such an important title. I cannot tell you how sorry I was to hear of your great trouble. Is there anything I can do? You have only to command me. Please see Mr Havelock and show him this letter. I have already written to him, authorizing him to pay you any money you may require."

Dick did not ask what the trouble had been. He guessed, from the black which Mrs Lansdown still wore, that her loss was a recent one.

"I did not see Mr Havelock, of course, though he very kindly wrote to me on receipt of Pierce's letter, offering his help. And now that I've satisfied your curiosity, Mr Martin, perhaps you will satisfy mine. What are these alarming instructions you give us, and why should we be prepared to leave town at any hour of the day or night?"

Sybil had been a silent but interested audience, but now she asserted her views.

"I'm sure Mr Martin wouldn't ask us to do anything that was absurd, mother," she said; "and if he wishes us to be ready to leave at a second's notice, I think we should do as he asks. It is in connection with the key?" She turned her grave eyes on Dick.

"Yes," he said, "and something else. As I say, I'm only groping for the moment. Certain facts are definitely established in my mind beyond question. But there are others which have got to be worked out."

He asked Mrs Lansdown if she had heard of Stalletti, but she shook her head.

"Do you know Mr Cody?" he asked, and she thought hard for a long time.

"No, I don't think I do," she replied.

13

A few minutes later Dick took his leave, and walked down towards Bedford Square. Once or twice he looked back. On the opposite side of the road a man was keeping pace with him about twenty yards to his rear. Immediately behind him was another saunterer. At the corner of Bedford Square a taxicab was waiting, and the driver hailed him urgently. But Dick ignored the invitation. He was taking no risks tonight. The two men he might deal with, but trouble awaiting him in a strange taxicab might be more difficult to overcome.

Presently he saw a taxi coming towards him, and, stopping the driver, got in and was driven to the Station Hotel. Through the glass at the back of the car he saw another taxi following him. When he paid off his own at the entrance of the hotel, he observed, out of the corner of his eye, the second taxi pull up some distance away and two men get out. Dick booked a room, gave the cloakroom ticket to a porter, and slipped through the side entrance which opens directly on to the station platform. A train was on the move as he emerged, and, sprinting along, he pulled open a carriage door and jumped in.

For all he knew, he might be in the Scottish express, whose first stop would be in the early hours of the morning somewhere in the neighbourhood of Crewe. But, fortunately for him, the train was a local one, and at Willesden he was able to alight and pay his fare to the ticket-collector. Diving down to the electric station, he arrived on the Embankment an hour after he had left the Lansdowns' flat.

Two hundred yards from the station is a grim building, approached under a covered arch, and this was Dick's destination. The constable on duty at the door recognized him.

"Inspector Sneed is upstairs if you want him, Mr Martin," he said.

"I want nobody else," said Dick, and went up the stone stairs two at a time.

Sneed was in his chair, an uninspiring man. The chief commissioner once said of him that he combined the imagination of a schoolgirl with the physical initiative of a bedridden octogenarian.

He sat as usual in a big armchair behind his large desk; a fire burned on the tiled hearth; a dead cigar was between his teeth, and he was nodding. He was at Scotland Yard at this hour because he had not had sufficient energy to rise from his chair and go home at seven o'clock. This happened on an average five nights a week.

He opened his eyes and surveyed the newcomer without any particular favour.

"I'm very busy," he murmured. "Can't give you more than a minute."

Dick sat down at the opposite side of the table and grinned.

"Ask Morpheus to put you down on your feet, and listen to this."

And then he began to talk, and almost at the first sentence the chief inspector's eyes opened wide. Before Dick Martin had been talking for ten minutes there was not a man in New Scotland Yard more wide awake than this stout, bald, thief-taker.

"You've got this out of a story-book," he accused, when Dick paused for breath. "You're passing across the latest mystery story by the celebrated Mr Doyle."

And then Dick went on with his narrative, and at the end Sneed pressed a bell. After a long time his sergeant came into the room.

"Sergeant," said Sneed, "I want one man at the front and one man at the back of 107, Coram Street. I want your best shadow to follow Mr Martin from tomorrow, and that man must sleep at Mr Martin's flat every night. Got that?"

The officer was jotting down his instructions in a notebook.

"Tomorrow morning get through to the Chief Constable of Sussex, and tell him I want to raid Gallows Cottage, Gallows Hill, at eleven-fifteen pip-emma. I'll bring my own men and he can have a couple of his handy to see fair play. That's about the lot, sergeant."

When he had gone, Sneed rose with a groan from his chair.

"I suppose I had better be getting along. I'll walk back with you to your flat."

"You'll do nothing of the kind," said Dick ungraciously. "To be seen out with you is like wearing my name and licence. I'll get back into the flat – don't worry."

"Wait a bit. Before you go – the fellow who attacked you in the drive at Gallows Cottage was a naked man, you say?"

"Nearly naked."

"Stalletti," mused the inspector. "I wonder if he's been up to his old tricks. I got him three months for that."

"What were his old tricks?" demanded Slick.

Sneed was lighting his cigar with slow, noisy puffs.

"Rearranging the human race," he said.

"A little thing like that?" said Dick sardonically.

"Just that." Sneed inspected the ragged end of his cigar with disfavour. "Got that weed from a man who ought to know better than try to poison the metropolitan constabulary," he said. "Yes, that was Stalletti's kink. His theory was that, if you took a baby of two or three years old, and brought it up wild, same as you'd bring up any other animal, you'd get something that didn't want clothes, didn't want to talk, but a perfect specimen of human. He reckoned that men ought to be ten feet high, and his general theory was that all the life-energy – that's the expression – that flows into human brains and human thought, ought to be directed to making muscle and bone. I guess you've come upon one of his experiments – I'll put him away for life if I find anybody in his house, dressed or undressed, who can't spell c-a-t, cat."

Dick left Scotland Yard by the Whitehall entrance, a cab having been brought from the Embankment, and he was set down at the loneliest part of the Outer Circle which encircles Regent's Park. By this time he knew that the janitor would be off duty and the entrance doors of the flats closed. The little street was deserted when he turned in, making a circuitous way through the mews at the back of the buildings. He opened the outer door, passed quickly up the stairs and into his apartment. He stopped long enough to shoot the bolts in the door, then, switching on the lights, he went from room to room and made a close inspection. Everything was as he had left it.

Before he had gone out that evening, he had drawn the heavy curtains over the windows of the room he intended using. He had lowered even the kitchen blind, so that, on his return (as he intended to return), no light could be seen by a watcher on the outside.

As he changed his coat for the old shooting jacket, he remembered, with a little grimace of disgust, the morning when he had found poor Lew. What had Lew seen in the tomb of the Selfords? What vault had he been asked to unlock in that "great hole dugge in the earth"?

He brewed himself a pot of coffee, and, putting on the table one of the six stout volumes that had come that afternoon, he began his search. The *London Gazette* is not exactly as amusing as a Molière comedy, but Dick found these pages, filled with records of bankruptcies and judgments, of enthralling interest. It was past two o'clock when he gathered his notes together, put them in a small safe, went into his bedroom and undressed.

Turning out the light, he pulled aside the curtains and, opening his window, looked out. A waning moon rode in a cloudless sky; a gentle wind was blowing, as he discovered when he got into bed, for it moved the dark blind so that a perpendicular streak of moonlight, which changed its shape with every movement of the blind, lay down the bedroom wall. Within a few minutes of punching his pillow into shape, Dick had fallen into a dreamless slumber.

He was the lightest of sleepers, and it seemed to him that he had hardly closed his eyes before he was wide awake again. What had disturbed him he could not remember. It might have been the flapping of the blind, but he decided that that was a noise which he had already discounted before he had gone to sleep. He lay on his left side, facing the door, which was flush with the wall against which the head of the bed rested. He must have been asleep for some considerable time, he decided, for the moonlight streak that had been over the bureau had now reached to within a foot of his bed, and lay exactly along the edge of the doorway. Even as he looked, he saw the door moving, slowly but certainly; and then there came into view, hideously clear in the moonlight, a hand. A hand, but such a hand as he had never seen before. The great thick fingers were like the tentacles of an octopus; blunt at their points, the skin about the knuckles wrinkled, the fat thumb squat. It was holding the edge of the door, pushing it slowly inward.

In a second he had rolled out of bed on the opposite side and dropped to the floor, as something big and heavy leapt on to the bed with a guttural inhuman cry that was terrible to hear.

As Dick dropped, his left hand thrust upward under the pillow and gripped the Browning that was there. So doing, his bare forearm touched for a second the back of a swollen hand, and he had for a moment a sense of physical sickness. Facing his unseen enemy, he reached back for the blind, and with one jerk tore it down. Instantly the room was flooded with moonlight. Save for himself, it was empty!

The door was wide open, and, changing his pistol hand, he reached round for the switch of the light that lit the hall. At a glance he saw that the front door was still locked and bolted, but the door of the kitchenette was wide open. So also was the window when he got there, and, bending over the iron rail of the balcony, he saw a shape scuttling down a rope ladder fastened to the balcony rail. As he searched the yard with his eyes, the figure vanished into the shadows.

He waited, listening, looking down into the mews, hoping to get another glimpse of his assailant. Then he heard the soft purr of a motor-car, that grew fainter and fainter, and presently passed from hearing.

Dick went into his study. The clock pointed to four, and in the east the sky was already paling. Who was this unknown murderer? He was satisfied that it was the same man who had attacked him at Gallows House.

He pulled up the rope ladder. It was an amateur affair, evidently home-made, for the rungs were of rough, unshaven wood, and the supporting rope hand-plaited. How they got on to the little balcony outside the kitchen door was a mystery, though he suspected that a stone attached to twine had been thrown over the projecting rail, and that first a cord and then a ladder had been pulled up. That this surmise was not far from the truth, he discovered when daylight came and he was able to search the courtyard below. Here he found cord and string, and to the latter was attached a small iron bolt. It was easy enough, now he came to examine the crime in the light of knowledge. By this way had come the murderer of Lew Pheeney. The back of Clargate Gardens looks on to a mews, from which there were two egresses, and only a wall need be surmounted to reach the paved courtyard immediately behind the flats; possibly not ten minutes had elapsed between the arrival of the assassin and that moonlight vision of his hideous hand.

Day had come now, and Dick was reeling with weariness. He threw himself down on the bed, half-dressed as he was, pulled the coverlet over him, and was immediately asleep.

14

It was the ringing of the telephone bell that woke him. He rolled over on the bed and took down the receiver.

"Hullo!" he said, in genuine surprise. "Your voice was the last in the world I expected to hear."

There was a little laugh at the other end of the phone.

"You recognized it? That's rather clever of you. I came down to see you half an hour ago, but the hall porter was certain that you were not in."

"Is anything wrong?" he asked quickly.

There was a little hesitancy.

"N-no," said Sybil Lansdown. "Only I wanted to – consult with you. That is the technical term, isn't it?"

"Come along by all means. I will mollify the porter."

She did not know why the porter should need mollification until she arrived. He had had no time to shave, to do any more than jump in and out of the bath, and he was in the throes of cooking when he opened the door to her.

"The truth is," he said, "I've sent my housekeeper away – that's rather a grand name for a daily help, but it impresses most people."

"Then I'll be impressed," she laughed, and sniffed. "What is that burning?"

He clasped his forehead and flew into the kitchenette, the girl at his heels.

"When you fry eggs," she said severely, "you usually put fat in the pan. You are not domestic, Mr Martin. And what on earth is that?"

She pointed to the crude rope ladder that lay in the corner of the kitchen.

"My fire escape," he said glibly. "I'm one of those scared folk who can't go to sleep unless they're sure that they're not going to be roasted – with or without fat," he added maliciously, "before they wake."

She was looking at him suspiciously.

"It never occurred to me that you were that kind of man," she said, and sliced the eggs scientifically from the pan on to a plate. "Twelve o'clock is disgracefully late for breakfast, but I'll wait till you have finished. You have just got up, I suppose? Did I wake you?"

"You did," he confessed. "Now, Miss Lansdown, what is troubling you?"

"Finish your breakfast," she ordered, and was adamant to his wheedling until he had drunk his coffee. "I was talking to mother last night after you'd left. I'm afraid you've rather worried her. And you need not feel penitent about it, because I realize that you only said as much as you thought necessary. We had a long, long talk, and the upshot of it was, I went to see Mr Havelock this morning, and I told him all about my Portuguese trip and the incident of the key. Mr Havelock was very worried, and he wants me to have police protection. In fact, I had the greatest difficulty in dissuading him from telephoning to Scotland Yard. I then made a suggestion to him, which rather surprised him, I think."

"What was the suggestion?"

"I won't tell you. I'd like to spring my surprise on you without warning. Have you a car?"

He nodded.

"Will it hold three?"

"Who is the other?" asked Dick, nettled at the thought that what at first had promised to be a *tête-à-tête* was to be spoiled by the inclusion of a third person.

"Mr Havelock. We are going down to Selford Hall – and the tombs of the Selfords," she added dramatically.

A slow smile dawned on Dick's face.

"You're certainly a mind-reader, for I was taking that trip this afternoon – alone."

"You wouldn't have been able to see the tombs alone," said the girl; "and I warn you it's an awfully creepy place. In fact, mother isn't particularly keen on my going down with you. Mr Havelock has very kindly agreed to come, and I'm relieved, because he knows the place and its history. We are to call for him at half-past two at his office. And will you bring the key you have?"

"The two keys," he corrected. "I'm sort of collecting keys just now. Yes, I'll be there."

She gathered up her bag and rose.

"What is the mystery?" he asked, sensing from her air of quiet triumph that she had made some important discovery.

"You will know this afternoon," she said.

He saw her from the door, took off his coat, and shaved, and by one o'clock he had retrieved the keys from his banker, and just before half-past one his car drew up at the door of 107, Coram Street. The girl was waiting for him, for no sooner had he knocked than the door opened and she appeared.

"Have you the keys?" she asked, almost before he had greeted her. "Mother doesn't like my going. She is nervous about anything connected with the Selford family."

"What is the mystery?" he asked.

"You shall see. I feel in my most mysterious mood. You haven't asked me why I'm not at the library. It is Founder's Day, and to celebrate the birth of the man who opened the library – we close it! Are you a good driver?"

"I have few equals," he admitted modestly.

"But are you a good driver?"

It was only then, as she chattered on inconsequently, that he realized that she was a little overwrought; perhaps some of her mother's nervousness had been communicated to her. Certainly, if she had a premonition of danger, that terrible day was to justify her fears. If Dick had half guessed what horrors lurked in the lap of that warm spring day, he would have driven the car into the nearest lamp-post.

The machine turned into Lincoln's Inn Fields and stopped before the Havelock building. When Mr Havelock came down to the car, he was smiling broadly, as though there were an element of humour in the adventure.

"How does it feel," he asked, as the car moved westward, "for a detective to receive a clue from an amateur? Are you very much chagrined at Miss Lansdown's remarkable theory?"

"I haven't heard the theory," said Dick, skilfully dodging between a bus and a taxicab. "I've got my thrill coming."

"I hope you will get it," said Havelock dryly. "Frankly, I would not have come on this little jaunt but for the fact that my monthly visit to Selford Hall is due, and a lawyer never loses an opportunity of saving unnecessary expenses. You, Mr Martin, will appear in the expense sheet of the Selford estate as a liability!"

Like other men whose jokes were infrequent, he was amused at the slightest of his own jests.

The car flew through Horsham, bore to the right on to the Pulborough Road, and, nearly two hours after they had left the City, it pulled up before a pair of imposing lodge gates. At the sound of the horn an untidy-looking woman came from the lodge, opened the gates, and dropped a curtsey to Mr Havelock as the car sped up a well-tended drive.

"We have to keep the place in spick and span order," explained Mr Havelock; "and one of my jobs is to engage a staff of servants the moment our globe-trotting young lord decides to settle down in his native land."

"Are there any servants in the hall itself?" asked Dick.

Havelock shook his head.

"A caretaker and his wife only," he said. "Once a month we have a contingent of women in from the village to clean up and dust and polish. As a matter of fact, the place is in a very good state of repair, and why he doesn't let it is beyond my understanding. By the way," he said suddenly, "I had a letter from him this morning. He is delaying his arrival till December, which probably means that he won't be home this winter."

"Where is he now?" asked Dick, looking over his shoulder.

Mr Havelock smiled.

"I shouldn't like to be very explicit on the subject. He *was* at Cairo when the Egyptian mail left. He's probably now in Damascus or Jerusalem. I don't mind confessing that I often wish him in Jericho!"

At that moment the Hall came into view; a Tudor house of severe and unpleasing lines. To Dick's untutored eye it had the appearance of a large brick barn, to which twisted chimneys and gables had been added. The car drew up at the broad gravelled space before the porch.

"We'd better get down here. We have a mile walk across the rough," said Havelock.

At the sound of the car wheels the caretaker, a middle-aged man, had appeared, and with him the lawyer exchanged a few words about the estate. It seemed that the caretaker was also acting as bailiff, for he reported a fence that needed repairing, and an oak that had been uprooted in a recent storm.

"Now, then," said Havelock. He had brought a walking-stick with him, and led the way across the broad lawn which, Dick noted, had recently been cut, through an orchard into a farmyard, which was untenanted save for half a dozen chickens and a dog, and through another gate into the park. Though there was no road, there was a definite pathway which led across the broad acres, skirting and half-encircling the steep bluff under which the house was built, through a spinney, and at last into a shallow valley, on the opposite side of which stood a long, dark line of trees.

As they climbed the gentle slope that led to the wood, Dick was struck by the lifelessness of the dark copse, which he would have recognized from Mrs Lansdown's description. The trees, with their green, dank-looking boles, seemed dead in spite of their new greenness. Not a leaf stirred upon that airless day; and to add to the gloom, a big thunder-cloud was rising rapidly beyond the bluff, showing defined edges of livid grey against the blue sky.

"It is going to rain, I'm afraid," said Mr Havelock, glancing up. "We're nearly there."

The path became visible again; it led a serpentine course through the trees, mounting all the time. And then, unexpectedly, they came into a clearing, in the middle of which was a great dome-shaped rock.

"This is called the Selford Stone," explained Mr Havelock, pointing with his stick; "and that is the entrance to the tombs."

Cut in the face of the rock was an oblong opening, covered by a steel grille, red with rust, but, as Slick saw, of enormous strength. Mr Havelock put down the lanterns he had been carrying, and lit them one by one before he took from his pocket a big, ancient-looking key, and inserted it in the rusty lock. With a turn of his wrist the ward snapped back and the door of the iron grille opened squeakily.

"Let me go first."

The lawyer stooped and went down a flight of moss-covered steps. The girl followed, Slick bringing up the rear. There were twelve of these steps, the detective counted, and by the light of a lantern he saw a small vaulted room, at the end of which was another steel grille of lighter make. The same key apparently fitted both.

Beyond the second door the solid rock had been hollowed out into twenty tiny chapels. They looked for all the world like refectory cells, with their heavy oaken doors and huge hinges, and on each had been carved a string of names, some of which, as Dick found when he tried to read them, were now indecipherable, where the wood had rotted.

The chapels ran along two sides of the narrow passage in which they stood, and at the very end was the twenty-first cell, which differed from all the others in that its door was of stone, or so it appeared at first glance. It differed, too, in another respect, as Dick was to discover. Mr Havelock turned to him and held up the lantern, that the visitor might better see.

"Here is what Miss Lansdown wishes you to see," he said slowly. "The door with the seven locks!"

Dick stared at the door. There they were, one under the other. Seven circular bosses on the door, each with its long key slit.

Now he knew. It was to this awful place that Lew Pheeney had been led to work under the fear of death!

The door was enclosed in a fantastic frame and gruesomely ornamented. A stone skeleton was carved on each pillar; so real they looked that even Dick was startled. He tapped the door with his knuckles; it was solid – how solid, he soon learned.

"Who is in here?" he said, and Havelock's finger pointed to the inscription:

"Sr HUGHE SELLFORDE, Kt
Fownder of ye Sellforde House.

Heare I wayte as quiet as a mouse
Fownder of the Sellforde House
A curse on whosoever mocks
Who lieth fast with seven lockes.
Godde have mercie."

"The inscription is of a much later period than Hugh's death," said Havelock.

"What is in there? Is he – buried here?" asked Dick slowly.

Mr Havelock shook his head.

"I don't know. The late Lord Selford, who had the old door with its seven locks taken down, and this new door – which is steel, by the way – made in Italy, said there was nothing except an empty stone casket; and, indeed, nothing can be seen."

"Seen?" repeated the girl in surprise. "How is it possible to see?"

There was a little panel about six inches in length and two inches broad, apparently part of the solid door, and running across its centre. Mr Havelock caught its bevelled edge between his finger and thumb and it moved aside, leaving a small aperture not an inch in depth.

"I ought to have brought an electric torch," he said.

"I've got one," said Dick, and, taking a small lamp from his pocket, he held it up near to his eyes and sent the light into the interior.

He looked into a cell about six feet square. The walls were green and damp; the rudely carved stone floor was thick with dust. In the very centre, resting on a rough stone altar, was an oblong, box-shaped sarcophagus of crumbling stone.

"The stone box? I don't know what that is," said Havelock. "Lord Selford found it in the tomb and left it as it was. There was no sign of a body – "

Suddenly the passage was lit by a blue, ghastly flame, that flickered for a second and was gone. The girl, with a gasp of fright, clung to Dick's arm.

"Lightning," said Havelock calmly. "I'm afraid we're going to have a wet journey back to town."

Even as he spoke, the hoarse roar of thunder shook the earth. It was followed by another flash of lightning, that revealed the ghostly doors of the dead on either side, and sent the girl shrinking against the detective.

"We'll not get wet, anyway," said Dick, patting the shoulder of the trembling girl. "There's a whole lot of nonsense talked about storms. They're the most beautiful demonstrations that nature sends. Why, when I was in Manitoba – "

The flash was followed instantly by a deafening explosion.

"Something's hit," said Dick calmly.

And then, from the far end of the passage, came the sound of the clanging of metal against metal.

"What was that?" he asked, and, flying along the passage, dashed through the outer lobby, up the slippery stairs to the entrance gates.

A flash of lightning blinded him for a second; the thunder crash that came on top of it was deafening; but he had seen what he had feared. The great iron grille had been shut on them, and on the wet clay before the door he saw the prints of naked feet!

15

Sybil and Havelock had followed closely behind him. Havelock's face had lost its rubicund colour, and the hand that went up to shake at the rail was trembling.

"What foolery is this?" he said angrily, and the quavering note may have been due to his annoyance.

Suddenly Dick's pistol leapt up. Twice he fired at the figure he glimpsed through the dripping rhododendrons. It had grown in a few minutes from bright sunlight to a gloom that was almost terrifying. The clouds sent the rain hissing in his face, but the flicker of lightning had given him a glimpse of the huge, fleshy arms.

"Oh, don't shoot; please – please don't!" The girl was sobbing, her head on his breast, and Dick dropped his pistol.

"You have a key to open the gate?" he asked in a low voice, and Havelock nodded.

"Give it to me."

Martin took the key from the shaking hand, put his arm through the bars and inserted it in the lock. A sharp twist of his wrist and the door was pushed open.

"Go on ahead; I won't be far behind you."

He dashed into the bushes where he had seen the figure, and he saw that he had not altogether failed, for on the long yellow cylinder that lay on the grass was a spatter of blood. He turned the cylinder over; it was about four feet in length and immensely heavy. Attached to the nozzle was a rubber tube about an inch in diameter. Searching round, he found a second cylinder, with a similar equipment. At the nozzle end of this latest find was a circular red label which had evidently been scratched off its fellow. "W D. Chlorine Gas. Handle Carefully. Poison." There was no sign of the half-naked man, and he started off at a run to overtake Sybil.

The lightning flashed incessantly, and there was scarcely an interval between the peals of thunder. Both the girl and Mr Havelock were as pale as death when he caught them up.

"What was it? Whom did you fire at?" asked Havelock huskily.

"Nerves," said Dick, without shame.

By the time they reached the house they were wet through, but he declined the invitation to go into the Hall and dry his clothes. He had work to do, and no sooner had the door closed on the girl than he was on his way back to the Selford tombs.

As he approached the wood he proceeded with caution, searching left and right and keeping his eyes on those little clumps of bushes which afforded cover. The wounded man was nowhere in sight.

He had slipped the key of the catacombs into his pocket, and now, having opened the grille, he took a pair of handcuffs from his hip pocket, snapped them at the top and bottom of the lock, so that it was impossible for the door to close. This done, he descended the steps, and, flashing his lamp before him, he came to the door of the seven locks. From an inside pocket of his waistcoat he took out the two keys and tried one of them on the top keyhole, without producing any result. It was not until he had got to the fourth slit that the key slipped in and turned with a click. He pulled gently, but the door did not budge. He tried with the second of the keys, and found that it fitted the last of the locks. Turning them both together, he pulled again, but the door did not move.

The mystery of the door was very clear to Dick Martin. Seven keys had to turn simultaneously before the door would open; and when it opened, what was there to see? He drew back the panel and looked at the stone urn. If the ancient Sir Hugh were buried here, was his body in that casket?

It was impossible to see the side walls in their entirety, but from what view he got it seemed unlikely that there could be any hidden sepulchre. The long shelf cut in the solid rock (which he now saw for the first time) had in all probability held all that was mortal of the first Selford, but no trace remained of him.

Pocketing the keys, he went back, closing and locking the middle door, and ascended the steps into the daylight. Here he had a shock. Not a dozen feet from the mouth of the tomb was one of the long yellow cylinders which he had last seen fifty feet away. The beast-man, then, was somewhere at hand; in all likelihood was watching him at this moment with hateful eyes. In spite of his self-possession, a little shiver ran down Dick Martin's spine.

There was something obscene about this strange visitant. He lifted the heavy cylinder, walked a few paces, and flung it into the bushes, and then followed the path through the trees.

He had an almost overpowering desire to run. He recognized with horror that he was on the verge of panic, and it needed but this discovery to swing him round to face the way he had come. Slowly, and against every natural instinct, he walked back through the forest towards where the cylinder was, to where his enemy was hiding. Coming to the edge of the clearing, he waited a full minute. Having thus tutored his nerves, he continued on his way to the house, never once looking back, but all his nerves taut.

It was with a feeling very much like relief that he reached the open valley and the comforting sight of the ugly home of the Selfords. The cold malignity of this inhuman creature; his persistence, wounded as he was, to destroy the man against whom his enmity had been roused; the deadly earnestness of him – all these things were impressive. This accidental association with the door of seven keys that hid nothing apparently but dust had brought him into deadly peril – had it also jeopardized Sybil Lansdown? At the thought, something gripped at his heart. It was all so unreal, so unbelievable.

A member of the everyday world who suddenly found himself in a community of pixies and fairies could be no more bewildered than was Richard Martin at the revelations which had followed one on the other during the past three days. Crime he knew, or thought he knew; and criminals were an open book to him. His youth had been spent amongst these evaders and breakers of the law. They had taught him their sinister tricks; he had become proficient in their practices. He knew the way their minds worked, and could – and would, since he was something of a writer – have prepared a passable textbook on criminal psychology.

But now he was out of the world of real crime. Only once before had he had that experience, when it was his duty to investigate a series of terrible accidents which had shocked Toronto to its depths. Here he had met for the first time the amateur criminal, and found himself at sea. But for the greatest good luck, the man he sought would have escaped detection. As it was, he virtually betrayed himself. The criminal mind is not a brilliant one; its view is commonplace, its outlook narrow and restricted. The average criminal lives meanly, from hand to mouth, and is without reserves, either of assistance in committing a crime or in covering his retreat.

Crime was an ugly word, he thought, as he paced slowly towards the house. Up to now, beyond the attempts which this unknown assailant of his had made, no charge could lie against any discoverable man. Except Lew Pheeney! Poor Lew, he had belonged to the real world. What agony of mind had he suffered when, in the dark of the night, he had found himself working on that awful door!

He was soaked to the skin, but was not aware of the fact until, with a gasp of dismay, the girl drew attention to his sodden coat just as he was taking his place at the wheel.

"Did you go back to look for the gate locker?" asked Mr Havelock, who had returned to his old buoyant manner.

"Yes," said Slick, as he started the car. "I didn't find him, though. Traces of him – yes, but not him."

"Was he wounded?" asked Sybil quickly.

"Well, if he was wounded, it wasn't serious," said Dick cautiously.

"I wish to heaven you had killed the brute," snapped Havelock viciously. "Br-r!"

He had borrowed an overcoat from the caretaker, and dozed in this all the way to town. They overtook and passed through a corner of the storm near Leatherhead. But the three people were too occupied with their own thoughts even to notice the incident. They put Mr Havelock down at his house in St John's Wood, and Sybil, who was feeling very guilty for having brought an elderly man on this unpleasant adventure, was suitably apologetic.

"It is nothing, and I'm really not so wet as our friend," said Mr Havelock good-humouredly. "And I'm certainly not worried about what we saw. It is what I didn't see that concerns me."

"What you didn't see?" repeated the girl.

Havelock nodded.

"Our friend has discovered a great deal more than he has told us, and I'm not so sure that the discovery is a pleasant one. However, we will talk about that in the morning."

He hurried into his house, and Dick turned the car towards Coram Street.

"I won't let you come in, Mr Martin," she said, when he set her down. "Will you promise to go straight home and take a hot bath and change your clothes at once?"

It was a promise easy to make, for his soul ached for the smell of hot water.

He was no sooner out of his bath and into dry clothes than he called up Sneed.

"I'm sorry to wake you up," said Dick exultantly, "but I wonder if you would come along and have dinner with me? I have three chapters to tell you."

Sneed grunted his dissatisfaction with the scheme, but after a while he agreed, though his promise was so vague and garnished with so many reservations that Dick was surprised when the bell rang and he opened the door to the big man, who walked wearily into the study and dropped into the first comfortable chair.

"Got the warrant for that raid tonight," he said. "We operate at ten o'clock."

"You told the Chief Constable of Sussex eleven-fifteen," said Dick, in surprise.

Inspector Sneed sighed.

"I want to get it over before the local Sherlocks arrive," he said. "Besides, somebody might tip off Stalletti. You never know. Trust nobody, Dick, not in our profession. I suppose you haven't spilt this story to anybody?"

Dick hesitated.

"Yes, I've told a little to Mr Havelock, and, of course, a lot to Miss Lansdown."

Sneed groaned.

"Havelock's all right, but the lady – oh, my heavens! Never trust a woman, my son. I thought that was the first article in a policeman's creed. She'll be having people in to tea and telling 'em all about it. I know women."

"Have you told anybody?" demanded Dick.

Inspector Sneed's smile was very superior.

"Nobody except the chief and my wife," he said inconsistently. "A wife's different. Besides, she's got toothache and she hates opening her mouth anyway. A woman with toothache never betrays a confidence. Make a note of that when you write your book."

It was the inspector's belief that every police officer in the force was secretly engaged in preparing his reminiscences; a delusion of his which had its justification in a recently printed series of articles that had appeared in a Sunday newspaper.

"Now, what have you got to tell me?"

He listened with closed eyes whilst Martin told him of the afternoon spent at the Selford tombs. When he came to the part where the iron grille had been locked on the party, Sneed opened his eyes and sat up.

"Somebody else had a key," he said unnecessarily. "Nothing in that vault, you say?"

"Nothing that I could see, except the stone casket," said Dick.

"Humph!" He passed the palm of his hand round his big face rapidly. "Seven keys," he mused. "Seven locks. Two you've got, five somebody else have got. Get the five – or, better still, blow in the door with dynamite."

Dick took out his long cigarette-holder and puffed a cloud of smoke to the ceiling.

"There seems hardly any excuse for that. I fiddled with one of the keyholes a little, and I can tell you it's a lock that the best man in the world won't be able to pick. Pheeney failed."

Sneed jerked up his head.

"Pheeney! Good Lord! I'd forgotten him! Let me have a look at the key."

Dick took it from his pocket and gave it to the stout man, who turned it over and over on the palm of his hand.

"I don't know one like that," he confessed. "Italian, you say? Well, possibly. You didn't see the barebacked lad?"

"I caught a glimpse of him. He's as quick and as slippery as an eel – poor devil!"

Inspector Sneed looked up sharply.

"You're in my way of thinking, eh? That this is one of Stalletti's experiments?"

He was very thoughtful and did not speak for a long time.

"The gas must have been there all the time. And, of course, they knew you were coming. And then, I have an idea, the presence of Havelock took them by surprise. It's only an idea, and I don't know why I think so."

He rose with difficulty.

"Well," he said, "we'll see tonight. Have your car but don't bring your gun, because you're not supposed to be present, and I'd hate for there to be any unofficial shooting."

16

At half-past nine that night Dick Martin's car pulled up by the side of the road half a mile short of Gallows Cottage, and, dimming his lights, he sat down to wait for the arrival of the police car. He heard the whir of it long before its bright head-lamps came into sight, and, starting up his engine, he waited for it to fly past before he followed. The car ahead slowed and turned abruptly into the drive, Dick's machine immediately behind. By the light of his head-lamps he saw that the hole under the hedge had been filled up.

The first car nearly collided with the thickset hedge where the little road turned towards the house, and the driver had a narrow squeak of slipping into the deep ditch that ran immediately under.

Gallows Cottage was in darkness, as it had been when Dick had come before. By the time he came up to Sneed, the inspector was knocking at the door, and three of the half-dozen men the car had contained were making their way to the rear of the premises.

The answer to the knock came quickly. A light showed in the transom above the door and it was jerked open. It was Stalletti, as sallow and grimed as ever. He stood there, a quaint and sinister figure, his stained hands stroking his long, black beard, whilst Sneed explained in a few words the object of this call.

"Oh yes, I now know you," said the man, apparently unperturbed by this array of force. "You are Sneed. And your friend behind you is the gentleman who lost his petrol the other night. How careless! Enter, my friends, to this home of science!"

He stood aside with an extravagant gesture of welcome, and the five men crowded into the hall.

"My drawing-room you would wish to see, I am sure?" said Stalletti, flinging open the door of the room in which he had received Dick.

"I'll see that workroom of yours," said Sneed, and, as the man was leading them to the back of the house: "No, not the place at the back – the one upstairs."

Stalletti shrugged his shoulders, hesitated for a second, and with another shrug led the way up the uncarpeted stairs, at the head of which was a small room, the door of which lie threw open as he was passing. A smaller flight led to a broad landing, on which were three doors. Dick and Sneed entered the room on the left. It was a poorly furnished room; an old truckle bed in the corner, a battered and grimy washstand, one leg of which had been broken and repaired, and a deep old arm-chair was all the furniture it contained.

The next room was evidently Stalletti's office and bedroom. It was overcrowded with furniture, and was in a state of disorder that beggared description. In one corner near the window was a tall nest of steel drawers. Stalletti pulled one open with an extravagant smile.

"You would like to see in the drawers?" he asked sardonically.

Sneed did not reply. He looked under the bed, opened a bureau, ordered the tenant of the house to unlock a cupboard, and directed his attention to the third room, which was also a bedroom, this with two beds, if a heap of old rugs in each corner could be so called.

"Ah, you are disappointed, my Sneed," said Stalletti, as they went down the stairs. "You expected to find some of your little babies here? Possibly you said to yourself, 'Ah, that Stalletti has been up to his old tricks, and is again trying to create big, strong, human men from the puny little things that will grow up to smoke cigarettes and study algebra.' Ach!"

"You're pretty talkative tonight, Stalletti."

"Should I not be?" asked the bearded man gaily. "It is so seldom I have a party. Realize, my friend, that I do not sometimes speak for weeks, or yet hear the sound of a human voice. I live frugally; there is no need for a cook, for I have raw food, which is natural in the carnivora. I hear your motor-cars spinning by, filled with flat-chested little men smoking cigarettes, and evil-thinking women, planning treacheries, and I am still gladder that I am a silent carnivore. Now, my laboratory."

He opened the door of the back of the house and showed a long room, which had evidently been built upon the cottage. There were only two windows to the place, and they were in the roof. There was a very large table, littered with papers and books in every modern language; two long shelves running down one side of the room, containing jars and bottles, no two of which were alike (Dick saw a soda-water bottle half-filled with a red fluid and corked with cotton-wool); a bench covered with recording instruments, scales, microscopes of varying sizes; an old, patched-up operating table, and a chest of shallow drawers containing surgical instruments; test-tubes by the hundred and, in a cleared space on the table, a dead rat, pinned out flat by its feet.

"Behold the recreation of a poor scientist!" said Stalletti. "No, no, my friend," as Sneed bent over the table, "our rat is dead. I do not vivisect any more because of your foolish laws. What pleasure is here you cannot conceive! Could you find happiness in a week's study of chemical reactions?"

"Who else is in the house, Stalletti?" asked Sneed.

Professor Stalletti smiled.

"I live alone; you have seen for yourself. Nobody comes here."

"Mr Martin heard a scream the night he came."

"Imagination," said Stalletti coolly.

"He was also attacked in the drive by a half-naked man. Was that imagination?"

"A typical case," said the doctor, meeting his eyes without flinching.

"Somebody else sleeps upstairs; you've beds for four people."

A broad smile wrinkled the yellow face.

"I never lose hope of friends coming to me, but, alas! they do not arrive. I am alone. Stay here for a week – a month – and see for yourself. Leave one of your so-clever officers to watch me. It should not be difficult to prove my loneliness."

"All right," said Sneed, after a pause, and, turning, walked out of the house.

The professor stood on the doorstep and watched the car till it disappeared, then, locking and bolting the heavy door, he went leisurely up the stairs to his room. Opening a drawer of his desk, he took out a long dog-whip and whistled the lash in the air. Then he crossed to the steel nest of drawers and pushed home the one that had come out – the only one, in fact, that would come out. Pressing one of the knobs of the false drawers, the whole of the front swung out like a door.

"Come to your bed. It is late," said Stalletti.

He spoke in Greek. The thing that was crouching in the darkness came shuffling forth, blinking at the light. It was more than a head taller than the bearded man, and, save for the ragged pair of breeches it wore about its waist, it was unclothed.

"Go to your room. I will bring milk and food for you."

Stalletti, standing at a distance from his creation, cracked his whip, and the big man with the blank face went trotting through the door across the landing into the room with one bed. Stalletti pulled the door tight and locked it; then he went down the stairs, through the laboratory, and out by a small door to the grounds at the back of the house. He still carried his whip and swung the lash as he walked, humming a little tune. He passed through a fringe of fir-trees and, stopping under a spreading oak, whistled. Something dropped from the bough above almost at his feet, and sat crouching, its knuckles on the ground.

"Room – milk – sleep," he said to the figure, and cracked his whip when the listening shape moved too slowly. At the snap of it the strange thing that had dropped from the tree broke into a jog-trot, disappearing through the laboratory door, and Stalletti followed at his leisure.

He went upstairs a little later, carrying two huge bowls of milk and two plates of meat on a tray. When he had fed his creatures and locked them in their dens, he went back to his workroom, dismissing slaves and detectives from his mind, utterly absorbed in his present studies.

17

Mr Havelock was reading a letter for the third time that morning. Twice he had consulted his managing clerk, and he was reading it for the third time when Dick Martin was shown in.

"I hope I didn't get you out of bed too early, Mr Martin, and I have to apologize for bringing you into this matter which ended, so far as you were concerned when you returned. I had this letter this morning; I'd like you to read it."

The letter was in writing which was, by now, familiar to Dick. It bore the address of a Cairo hotel.

"Dear Havelock (it began),

"I had your cable about Dr Cody, and I am writing at once to tell you that I certainly know this man and I have had correspondence with him, so why he should deny all acquaintance with me, I can't understand, unless it is the natural reticence of a man who may not want other people to know his business. Cody wrote to me a long time ago, asking me for a loan. It was for a very considerable sum – £18,000 – and I had no inclination to advance this amount to a total stranger. He told me he had got into a very bad state, and that he wished to clear out of England, to get away from a man who had threatened to kill him. I forget the whole story now, but it struck me at the time that the man was sincere. I wish you would send me £25,000 in French notes. Register the parcel as usual, and address me at the Hotel de Paris, Damascus.

I hope to go on to Bagdad, and thence into Southern Russia, where I believe there is a big property to be bought for a song."

The letter was signed "Pierce."
"Do you usually send him money when he asks for it?"
"Invariably," said the other, in a tone of surprise.
"And you are sending him this large sum?"
Mr Havelock bit his lip.
"I don't know. I'm rather troubled about the matter. My managing clerk, in whose judgment I have complete faith, advises me to cable his lordship asking him to appoint another agent. The responsibility is too big, and after yesterday's horrible experience, I am almost inclined to wash my hands of the matter. It would, of course, mean a heavy loss to us, because the management of the Selford estates brings us in nearly five thousand pounds a year."

Dick was staggered at the figure.

"It must be an enormously wealthy estate," he said.

"It is," agreed Havelock. "And, unfortunately for me, it is increasing in value every day. It will soon become unwieldy."

"Did Lord Selford leave anything in the nature of a treasure?" asked Dick, as he remembered a question he had intended asking.

Havelock shook his head.

"No, beyond the cash at the bank, which was a large sum – fifty thousand pounds or so – there were no fluid assets. But he left a number of undeveloped coal lands in Yorkshire and Northumberland, which have since proved very valuable; in addition to which he had several large properties in Australia and South Africa, which have also enhanced in value to an enormous extent. You are thinking about the door with the seven locks?" he smiled. "Believe me, there is nothing there so far as I know, and I have seen every document, private and general, which the late Lord Selford left. That little cell is as much a mystery to me as it is to you. It could be cleared up in twenty-four hours if I had his lordship's permission to force the door. But I have never asked for it, because I have never seen the necessity for it." Then he smiled. "I have been hearing stories about you, Mr Martin. They tell me that you can pick a lock as skilfully as any cracksman."

"Most locks," said Dick promptly, "but none of the seven. I realize my limitations. Now, I could open that safe" – he pointed to a little black safe standing in the corner of the room – "as easily as I could open your office door. I won't say I could do it with a hairpin, but I have half a dozen instruments at home that would make that receptacle about as valuable a store as a cardboard box. But I've got a kind of instinct that tells me when I'm beaten, and I know I'm beaten on those seven locks. Has Lord Selford any relations?" he asked abruptly.

Havelock nodded.

"One," he said. "Miss Sybil Lansdown, and, of course, her mother, though in law Miss Lansdown would be regarded as the heir to the property, supposing Lord Selford died without issue."

He took up the letter from the table, and his eyes ran over the written page.

"I'm almost inclined to send you to Damascus with the money," he began, but Dick shook his head.

"No, sir." He was emphatic. "I've had one chase after this young man, and that is enough to last me for a lifetime. During the years he's been abroad has he received much money from you?"

"The greater part of five hundred thousand," replied Havelock quietly. "Generally for the purchase of estates, the deeds of which have never come to me. I have complained about this once or twice, but he has assured me that the title deeds were in good keeping."

"One question I want to ask you before I go," said Dick, after turning the matter over in his mind. "Is it possible that these letters are forgeries?"

"Absolutely impossible," replied Havelock. "I know his handwriting and its peculiarities as well as – indeed, better than – I know my own. I can assure you that not two years ago he wrote one of the letters I have in my file under my own eyes."

"He could not be impersonated?"

"Absolutely not. He is rather a thin-faced, sandy-haired man, who speaks with a little lisp. And the better to identify him, he has a round red patch – a birthmark – on his cheek, just below his ear. I have thought of all these possibilities. He might be impersonated, he might be held to ransom, or have fallen into the hands of some unscrupulous gang which was bleeding him. In fact, if I had not seen him at intervals during the past years, I should have become seriously alarmed. But there it is! If he chooses to wander about the world, I have no power to stop him, and his hobby is not so reprehensible that I can invoke the aid of the law to pin him down in England and keep him here. You are sure you would not like to take the trip to Damascus?"

"Perfectly sure," answered Dick immediately. "I can think of nothing I want to do less!"

Two disturbing factors had come into the life of Sybil Lansdown, and she found it difficult to concentrate her mind even upon rare editions or those inanimate volumes which once had seemed so interesting.

In one case the library helped to enlarge her knowledge. She collected all the literature available upon the history of the old county families, but there was little about Selford, except in one volume, written by a priest, which told, in too lurid detail, the story of Sir Hugh's many sins Sybil closed the book hastily when it became a little too detailed.

"I'm afraid we are not a nice family," she said, as she put the volume back on its high shelf.

There was nothing in the library that could help her unravel her feelings about Mr Martin. Sometimes she thought she liked him very much indeed; at other times she was equally certain that he annoyed her. She wished she had not gone to the Selford tombs, and that there had been no cause for her laying her head on his breast, or fluttering to his arms in a panic induced by ghastly carvings and a fortuitous flicker of lightning.

Women were very rare visitors to the library, and when, in the slackest part of the afternoon, a lady walked into her room she was a little astounded. A short, stout woman, with a face which did not err on the side of softness, she was expensively dressed, though her voice belied her elegant appearance, for it was a little coarse and somewhat strident.

"Are you Miss Lansdown?" she asked.

Sybil rose from her chair.

"Yes, I am Miss Lansdown. Do you want a book?" she asked, thinking, as was sometimes the case, that the woman had called on behalf of one of the subscribers.

"No, I don't read books," was the disconcerting reply. "A lot of rubbish and nonsense, that put ideas in people's heads — that's what books are! If *he* didn't read so much, he'd be a cleverer man. Not that he isn't a gentleman born and bred," she added hastily, "and a nicer gentleman to deal with I've never known. You can take it from me, miss, that that man couldn't think wrong. He may have made a mistake — we're all liable to make mistakes. But he's not the sort of man who'd put his 'and to anything that wasn't fair and square."

Sybil listened in astonishment to this mysterious paean of praise, directed she knew not whither.

"Perhaps your — er — "

"My husband," said the lady with dignity. "I am Mrs Bertram Cody."

Sybil's mind flew over the index of members without recalling anybody who bore that name.

"Dr Cody's wife," said the woman. "Have you got a chair where I can set down?"

With an apology, Sybil drew a chair forward and placed it for the visitor.

"My husband knew your father very well, miss. In fact, they were good friends years and years ago. And he said to me this morning — my husband, I mean: 'If you're going to town, Elizabeth, you might pop in at Bellingham's Libr'ry,' and he gave me the address; I've got it written down on a bit of paper."

She searched a very expensive bag and produced a small card.

"Yes, there it is, in his own 'andwriting."

She showed the girl a scrawl which told her nothing.

"My husband said: 'Go in and see Miss Lansdown and ask her if she'll come down to tea, and I can tell her something very interesting about her father that she never knew before.'"

Sybil was puzzled but interested. Who this strange woman was, and what position her husband occupied in society, she could only guess from the prefix the proud wife had put to her husband's name. As though she read the girl's thought, Mrs Cody went on: "He's not a medical doctor. A lot of people think he is, but he's not. He's a literary doctor."

"Oh, a doctor of literature?"

"And law." The lady nodded impressively. "He got it out of a college in America. The point is, miss, you have got lots of enemies." Mrs Cody lowered her voice until it was a harsh whisper. "My husband said: 'See the young lady and ask her not to breathe a word of what I've said, because it may cost me dear – it may cost me dear.'" She repeated the words slowly and imposingly. "'Take the Rolls-Royce,' he said, 'and maybe you can persuade her to come down and have a cup of tea. It wouldn't take her an hour, and nobody would know she'd been.'"

"But why shouldn't people know I've been?" asked the girl, secretly amused, and yet with a feeling at the back of her mind that there was something more serious in this communication than she could for the moment see.

"Because," said Mrs Cody, "of these enemies. They're not only after you, miss" – her voice was very solemn, and, in spite of her amusement, Sybil was impressed – "but they're after that Canadian man, the policeman."

"You mean Mr Martin?" asked the girl quickly.

Again Mrs Cody nodded her head.

"That's the fellow – the detective. They tried to get him once, but perhaps he hasn't told you about it. The next time he'll be popped off, as sure as my name's Elizabeth."

There was a telephone on the table, and Sybil looked at it for a moment in doubt.

"What had my father to do with all this?" she asked.

Mrs Cody pursed her lips, as though she could tell if she would.

"My husband will tell you that, miss," she said.

Sybil examined the woman more critically. She was undoubtedly the most commonplace individual she had met for a long time; but her wealth was advertised by an abundance of jewellery. For with every movement of her head two big diamond earrings winked and sparkled in the afternoon sunlight. Her fingers were scarcely visible under the rings that covered them, for she wore no gloves, and across her ample bosom was a huge diamond brooch.

"How far is it?" asked Sybil.

"Less than an hour. It's in Sussex." She explained the route and the exact situation of the house. "If you could get away in time for a cup of tea – "

"I could do that," said the girl thoughtfully, "for this is my early afternoon."

Mrs Cody consulted a jewelled watch.

"I'll wait for you," she suggested. "You'll find my Rolls-Royce" – she rolled the words sonorously – "waiting in the square. You can't mistake it. It's black, picked out with little red lines."

"But please don't wait. I shall be half an hour yet."

"I don't mind waiting. But I think I had better stay in the car till you come. You're going to have a big surprise, young lady, and you'll thank me until your dying day that my husband sent me to see you."

Sybil called up her flat, but her mother was out, and she remembered that Mrs Lansdown had gone to a bridge party – her one recreation. She called Dick Martin, with no better result; and at four o'clock she went out into the square and looked for the limousine. She had not far to look; a handsome car was drawn up near the kerb, and at her appearance moved slowly towards her. The chauffeur, a round-faced, young-looking man of thirty (she guessed) was dressed in sober livery. Mrs Cody opened the door for her, and she got into an interior that was so heavily perfumed that she mechanically turned the lever that lowered the windows.

"I hope you telephoned to your mother, my dear?" said Mrs Cody, with a sidelong glance at the girl.

"I did, but she was not at home."

"Then you left a message with the servant?"

Sybil laughed.

"We do not support such a luxury, Mrs Cody," she said. "Mother and I do the work of the house ourselves."

Mrs Cody sighed.

"You told somebody else where you were going, I hope, my dear? You should always do that when you're going out, in case of accidents."

"No, I told nobody. I tried to get – a friend on the phone, but he was out too."

For a second the ghost of a smile dawned on the hard face and vanished again.

"You can't be too careful," said the lady sententiously. "Do you mind setting back, Miss What's-your-name, in the corner. It's more comfortable."

It was also more unobservable, but this Sybil did not notice.

18

Soon they were speeding in a south-westerly direction, and although Mrs Cody was not an entertaining hostess, the girl found plenty to think about, and certainly did not resent the silence of this over-dressed woman. In less than an hour the car swung through a pair of heavy iron gates, up a long avenue, and stopped before a medium-sized house.

Sybil had never met the stout and smiling man who came to meet her.

"Ah! So this is the daughter of my old friend!" he said, almost jovially. "Little Sybil! You don't remember me, of course?"

Sybil smiled.

"I'm afraid I don't, Dr Cody," she said.

"You wouldn't, my dear, you wouldn't." His manner was paternal, but Mrs Cody, who knew her husband much better than most people, and who could detect his most subtle nuances of tone, shot one cold, baleful glare in his direction that was eloquent of her experience.

If Cody saw her, his manner certainly did not change. He took the girl's arm, much against her will, and led her into the handsome library, fussing over her like an old hen with a chick. She must have the best chair and a cushion for her back.

"Tea at once, my dear. You must be tired after your journey."

"I ham," said Mrs Cody emphatically. "I'd like a word with you, C."

"Certainly, my dear. Are you quite comfortable, Miss Lansdown?"

"Quite," said the girl, finding it difficult not to smile as she saw Mrs Cody flounce out with a red face and slam the door behind her.

In the hall the chauffeur was lighting a cigarette. He glanced round at the woman as she came out.

"Who's she, aunty?" he asked.

Mrs Cody shrugged her ample shoulders.

"She's the girl the old man was telling you about," she said shortly. "You ask too many questions; he's been complainin' about you."

"I thought she was." He ignored the complaint. "Not a bad-looker. I'm surprised at you leaving them two alone!"

"Never mind what you're surprised at," she said tartly. "Go and put that car in the garridge, and come and see me when it's done."

"There's plenty of time," answered the dutiful nephew coolly. "What's the old man going to do?"

"How do I know?" she snapped.

But he was in no way abashed.

"Has she got the key?"

"Of course she hasn't got the key, you fool!" she stormed. "And don't stand there asking me silly questions. And don't poke your nose into my business. And what do you know about keys?"

Her nephew looked at her meditatively.

"You're a queer couple, you and him," he said. "But it's no business of mine. That girl's certainly a good-looker. I'm going through to the kitchen to have some tea. The old man's given cook and Mrs Hartley a holiday, and the maid's away sick. It's rum that they should all be away together!"

He was strolling to the front door when he spoke, and now he turned back.

"Got everybody out of the house." He frowned. "What's the great idea, aunt?"

"Not so much 'aunt'. I'm 'missus' to you, you gaol-bird! I've told you about that before." She was trembling with fury, and he knew her well enough to realize that this was not a moment to provoke her to further anger. For seven years (with a pleasant interregnum) he had preserved the polite fiction of being a pampered menial in the house of Mrs Cody. His wages were good; he knew a little of the private affairs of the widow whom Dr Cody had most unexpectedly married, and for the consideration he received in the shape of a good bed, an excellent allowance, plus the assistance he had in the garage, he was quite willing to be blind to many curious happenings that he had witnessed in that house.

He walked towards his aunt, his cigarette drooping from his big mouth.

"What time am I taking that girl back to town?" he asked.

"She's staying here; you needn't bother."

He looked down at the floor, up at the ceiling, everywhere except at the woman, and then: "Does she know she's staying here?"

"Mind your own business."

"This is my business for once," he said obstinately. "I don't know who she is or what she is; if there's any monkey game going on, I'm not in it. I'll have the car ready to take her back in an hour."

The woman did not answer him. She walked rapidly across the hall and passed up the stairs out of sight. He waited till she had disappeared from view on the landing, and then he went out to the kitchen to his own tea and to meditate upon the strangeness of life at Weald House and the queer fate which, twelve years before, had turned his aunt from a household drudge to a lady of fortune.

It was Mrs Cody who eventually brought in the tea, placed it on the table, and immediately retired. Sybil saw nothing strange in this, thinking that her host had something to say which he did not wish to tell her before his wife. Three times she had made an ineffectual attempt to bring the conversation round to her father and the secret which Mr Cody had to reveal, but on each occasion he skilfully led the talk in another direction. But now, after a pretence of taking refreshment, the girl brought the matter to a head by bluntly asking what he had to tell.

"Well, young lady," Mr Cody coughed, "it's a very long story, and I doubt if I can tell you everything in the time we have. Would it not be an excellent idea if I got on to the telephone to your dear mother and asked her to come down and spend an evening with us?"

The girl looked at him in astonishment.

"I'm afraid that plan would not work. Mother and I are going to a theatre tonight," she said.

Sybil was ordinarily a very truthful person, but even very truthful people may be permitted to invent excuses for avoiding disagreeable experiences.

"May I not telephone and ask her?"

Knowing that her mother would not be back at the flat for another hour, she agreed. He went out of the room and was gone five minutes. When he returned, a broad smile suffused his face and he was rubbing his hands.

"Excellent, excellent!" he said. "Your dear mother has promised to come down this evening. I am sending the car for her. She says she can exchange the theatre tickets for another night."

Sybil listened, petrified with amazement, and into her annoyed amusement there crept a cold thread of fear. The man was lying. The theatre engagement had been invented on the spur of the moment, and her mother was not at the flat, she well knew. Danger! As if a red light had flashed before her eyes she saw it. There was some terrible peril threatening her, and she must temporize.

"I'm so glad," she said, with a calmness she did not feel. And then, in an easy conversational voice: "You have a very pretty house here, Mr Cody."

"Yes, it is a gem," he said complacently. "Would you like to see over it? It has a remarkable history. Originally a dower house, in the gift of a relative of yours – Lord Selford. I leased it many years ago – "

"You know Mr Havelock, don't you?" she said in surprise.

"Hum!" He fingered his chin. "No, I cannot say that I know Mr Havelock very well. I have done business with him; in fact, I once bought an Australian property from him. But in the present case the house was leased to me through a third person, and I very much doubt whether Mr Havelock is aware that I am the leaseholder. Do you know him well?"

"Slightly," she said. All the time her busy brain was working. What should she do? She wanted an excuse for seeing the grounds. A main road passed near the entrance lodge, and she knew there was a village close at hand. Once she was on the road, there would be sufficient excuses to take her into the village and the protection which such a community would offer her.

"You would like to see some of our rooms?"

"No, I don't think so. I would like to see your grounds. I thought I saw a bed of narcissi near the lodge," she said, and rose from her chair, her knees trembling.

"Hum!" said Mr Cody again. "Yes, it is a beautiful spot, but the ground is rather damp for you."

"I would like to go out," she insisted.

"Very good. If you will wait till I have had my second cup of tea." He busied himself with the tray and the teapot. "By the way, you haven't finished yours, and it is cold. Shall I pour you out another?"

"No, no, that will be sufficient, thank you."

What a fool she had been! To accompany a strange woman – a woman against whom every instinct warned her – to an unknown house. Nobody knew whither she had gone.

She took the cup from him, steeling her nerves to steady her hand, drank a little, and was grateful for the liquid, for her mouth had become dry and her throat parched with the consciousness of her position. It was not nice tea, she noticed, there was a salty, metallic taste to it, and with a little grimace she put down the cup.

"Thank you, that is enough," she said.

Perhaps it was the acute tension of the moment which left that queer after-taste in her mouth. She had noticed once before in her life how sensitive the palate becomes in a crisis of fear.

In one corner of the library was a small coat rack, and Mr Cody went leisurely to get his cap. When he looked round, Sybil was holding on to the edge of the table, her face white as death, her eyes glazed. She tried to speak, but could not form the words. And then, as he came to her, she collapsed in his arms.

He half-carried, half-dragged her to the sofa, and putting a cushion beneath her head, walked out of the library, locking the door behind him.

19

The round-faced chauffeur was standing in the open doorway, smoking.

"Where is Mrs Cody?" asked Cody sharply, his face going dark at the sight of the man's insolent indifference.

"Upstairs."

"Go and tell her I want her."

"Go and tell her yourself," said the man, without troubling to turn his head.

Cody's face went purple. It was evident that this was not by any means the first of their encounters. He mastered his rage with an effort, and, in a milder tone: "Go down to the village for me, will you, Tom? I want some postage stamps."

"I'll be going down later," said Tom, unmoved by this olive-branch. "Where is that girl?"

"Girl? Which girl?" asked the other, in a tone of innocent surprise.

"The girl you had in to tea. Don't tell me she has just gone out, because I've been standing here for ten minutes, and I heard you talking when I was in the hall."

Mr Cody drew a long breath.

"She's resting. The young lady is not very well. I've given her treatment – "

"Oh, shut up!" said the other contemptuously. "You ain't a medicine doctor, you're a doctor of laws – and Gawd knows some of 'em want doctorin' from what I've seen of 'em! When's she going home? I've got the machine ready."

"She may not go home tonight, Tom." Mr Cody was mildness itself now. "It was arranged that she should stay tonight."

Tom scratched his cheek irritably.

"She didn't know anything about it," he said. "When she got out she asked me if there wasn't another way back to town, because she wanted to call in to see a friend."

This latter was sheer mendacity on the part of Tom Cawler, and it was a slight coincidence that Mr Cody had been twice deceived in half an hour.

"She's not well, I tell you," he said sharply. "And whilst we're on the subject, your place is in the kitchen. I've stood about as much of you as I'm likely to stand, Cawler. You don't think because I married your aunt that you own this place, do you? Because, if that's your idea, you're going to get a shock. I've endured quite enough insolence from you, and you can go."

Tom nodded.

"I know I can go," he said. "Because why? Because nobody could stop me if I wanted to go. I could go this very minute if I liked – I don't like! This is a good job and I'm not going to lose it. I don't know what your dirty business is –"

Mr Cody exploded with anger.

"You – you scoundrel!" he spluttered. "You dare accuse your aunt of being –"

"I've got a great respect for my aunt." Tom Cawler was still staring at the ground. "I owe a lot to my aunt. I got all my crook blood from her side of the family, and you couldn't lay out any scheme for getting money quick that I wouldn't think she had a hand in." He glowered at the man for a second and then his eyes dropped.

"Yes, she's been a good aunt to me, Cody! Ever heard tell of my twin brother Johnny? I've been dreaming about him lately. I see him as plain as if he was standing before my very eyes. And I was only seven when he went away –"

"When he died," suggested Cody with unexpected mildness.

"Yuh – when he died. We used to sit under a tree in Selford – I was brought up on this estate – and sing 'Poor Jenny is a-weepin'.' Seven years."

His eyes, raised suddenly, were like burning fires, and the little man wilted under the gaze.

"Good kind aunt! I've seen her lick that little boy till he couldn't stand. She's lucky to be a woman. You tell her that one day. If she'd 'a' been a man, she'd have got hers long ago. I'm going round to get that car ready. You have that young lady waiting for me when I come back." There was menace in his tone which was unmistakable.

Without another word he lurched off, his hands in his pockets, a cigarette still drooping limply, and, turning, Mr Cody flew up the stairs and burst into the room where his better half was sitting. He slammed the door behind him, and for ten minutes there was the sound of angry voices. Presently Mrs Cody came out alone, and, going downstairs, unlocked the library and went in.

Sybil Lansdown was sitting up on the sofa, her head between her hands. Without a word, the woman gripped her arm and supported her out of the room and up the stairs. From this floor two flights of narrow stairs led, in one case to the servants' quarters, and in the other to a spare bedroom which was used also as a box-room, and it was into this apartment that the girl was pushed.

Sybil was almost unconscious. She never recalled that journey up the stairs. When she woke, with a splitting headache, she was lying on a small iron bed that sagged in the middle. A little wax nightlight was burning under a glass, for by this time the light was fading from the sky.

She sat up, her head reeling, and tried hard to think consecutively. Near the bed was a small table with a glass of water and two tiny pellets, which she might have ignored, but the aspirin bottle stood open beside them. Her head was splitting. Oblivious to danger, and realizing in a dull way that these were intended to counteract the effect of the drug she had taken, she swallowed the two pellets and drank every drop of the water without taking the glass from her lips.

With a groan she lay down on the bed, covering her eyes with her hands, and was sensible enough to make her mind as much of a blank as her throbbing brain would allow until the restorative took effect.

It was half an hour before the pain ceased and she ventured to lift her head again. She was dizzy, and with every movement the room swam round and round. But after a while she grew calmer, more her normal self, and she could think consecutively.

There was only a tiny window, and that was a skylight in the sloping roof. It was padlocked and covered with a stout wire netting. She tried the door, without expecting that her attempt to leave the room by that way would be of any avail. Going back to the bed, she sat down and tried hard to review her position without allowing her terror to overcome her.

She must have been mad to have gone alone with that woman (to that vain conclusion she naturally returned), but she was so confident of herself, and the counsel of perfection was very hard to follow, even in the most perfect of beings. The excuse was so flimsy, she told herself. Not a London child would have been deceived by this promise of family revelations. She dared not let herself think of her mother.

She tried the door again. It was heavily locked and probably bolted as well, for it resisted her strength at every point of its surface. It was very old and had the appearance of being something of a misfit, for there was a gap of an inch and a half between its bottom and the floor.

She walked back to the bed and sat down, trying to order her thoughts. The key! Was her detention remotely connected with that strip of steel? She was puzzled, but she would not allow herself to be utterly bewildered. She argued, as coldly as the circumstances would allow her, that, for some reason which she could not define, the key had something to do with her tragic situation.

She pulled up a chair and, mounting it, reached up to the skylight, but it resisted all her efforts, and, supposing she could force the window, it was utterly impossible that she could displace the three iron bars which covered the window.

As she was standing on the chair, she heard a footstep in the passage, firm and heavy, and, getting down to the floor, she turned to face the man who came in. It was some little time before the door was opened. As she rightly surmised, it was fastened with bolts, and these had to be shot before, with a click, the key turned and Cody came in.

He was one large, affable smile.

"My dear young lady, I'm afraid you have had a bad time. Do you have these attacks very often?"

"I don't know what attacks you mean, Dr Cody," she answered steadily.

"Very sad, very sad," he murmured, shaking his head mournfully. "I was really afraid for your life. Is there insanity in your family?"

The audacity of the question took her breath away.

"I don't suggest there is," he went on, "only I must say that your conduct is a little strange. You probably remember your screaming fit. No? Ah, I did not expect you would. It was very lamentable."

"Mr Cody" – she tried to keep her voice even, but it required a great effort – "I want to go home to my mother."

He looked hard at her for a long time.

"I suppose you do," he mused. "I suppose you do. But you need have no fear, my dear young lady; your mother has been notified and is already on her way."

There was a little table in the corner of the room, and he drew it to the centre and put down upon it the small black portfolio he was carrying under his arm. From this he took a folded sheet of paper, smoothed it gently, took out his fountain pen, unscrewed the top and fixed it.

"The position," he began, in his old oracular manner, "is a little irregular. It is not customary for me to receive young ladies who fall into hysterics, and I confess that I was considerably alarmed – my dear wife is prostrate with anxiety. She said, and very rightly: 'The position is a very awkward one for you, Bertram. Suppose this young lady suggests that you administered to her some noxious drug, and that you are detaining her against her will – although you and I are well aware that her illness was brought about by – um – natural causes, a censorious world may well look sceptically upon our explanation.'"

Sybil waited, knowing full well that, if Mrs Cody had made any kind of speech, it would not have been in those terms.

"Therefore, it has occurred to me," Mr Cody went on, "that it would be an excellent idea if you, of your own free will, made a statement to this effect, that I, Bertram Cody, Doctor of Literature and Law, have behaved with the greatest kindness and propriety, and that I placed you in this locked room only for one purpose – namely, to restrain you from doing a serious injury to yourself."

She glanced at the paper on the table.

"I can hardly confess that I'm mad," she said, with a half-smile.

"I do not expect you to do that," said Mr Cody hastily. "That reference to your condition of mind does not appear in this document. It is merely a – um – certificate of my probity, very dear to me. A mere whim of mine, but I am a whimsical person." He smiled broadly, picked up the pen, gave it to her.

"Can I read the document?" she asked.

"Is it necessary?" He was almost reproachful. "If you will sign this, I will see that you are conducted at once to your mother."

"You told me my mother was on her way," interrupted Sybil suspiciously.

"My idea," the man went on, calmness itself, "was to meet her halfway. I have telephoned, asking her to stay at the Mitre Inn, Dorking."

He handed the pen to the girl, and again she hesitated. The document was written on a quarto sheet and was closely typewritten. His large hand covered the paper, leaving her only the space to write. She was anxious to be gone, and, in her fear, clutched at any hope of freedom. The point of the pen had touched the paper when she saw a line visible through his extended fingers which arrested her movement.

"Should the said Sybil Ellen Lansdown predecease the said Bertram Albert Cody..."

"What is this paper?" she asked.

Sign it!" His voice was harsh, his manner changed as suddenly as a tropical sky.

"I shall not sign any document that I haven't read," she replied, and laid down the pen.

The smile left his face hard and menacing.

"You will sign that, or, by God, I'll – "

He checked himself with an effort, and strove again to recover the appearance of geniality.

"My dear young lady," he said, with a queer admixture of irritation and blandness, "why trouble your pretty little head about the wording of legal documents? I swear to you that this letter merely exculpates me from any – "

"I will not sign it," she said.

"You won't, eh?"

He gathered up the document and thrust it into his pocket. She shrank back as he advanced towards her. Suddenly she darted to the door and tried to pull it open. Before she could succeed, he had caught her by the waist and flung her back.

"You'll wait here, my young lady, till you change your mind. You will wait without food. If I had my way, without sleep. I've given you a chance for your life, you poor fool, and you haven't had the sense to grasp it. Now you can stay here until you recover your reason!"

In another second he had passed through the door, slamming it after him. She heard the bolts shot home with a sinking heart.

For a time she was too paralysed by her discovery to make any fresh attempt to escape. But after a while she took hold of herself and regained a little of her self-possession, though she so trembled that, when she stood upon the chair to try the skylight again, she could scarcely maintain her balance.

When she saw that escape by that way was impossible, she made preparations to keep the door against an intruder. She tried to pull the bed from the wall, but it was a heavy oaken affair and beyond her strength. A rickety washstand was the only prop she could find, and the back of this she wedged beneath the door handle and sat down to wait.

Hour followed hour, and there was no sound in the house, and at last, overcome by weariness, she lay down on the bed and, in spite of all her efforts to keep awake, was soon fast asleep.

She woke with a wildly beating heart and sat up. She had heard a sound in the passage outside; a shuffling, stealthy sound, which her guardian senses had heard in her deepest slumber. What was it? She listened, and for a long time there was nothing to break the silence. Then, from somewhere below, she heard a dull crash, as though something heavy had fallen. She listened, her hand on her heart, striving to check her racing pulse.

"Ow-w-w!"

She shuddered and almost fainted with horror. It was a squeal she heard, the squeal of a terror-stricken animal — another, deeper, guttural, horrible!

She listened at the door, her senses tense, and heard a faint, deep sobbing, then heard no more. Ten minutes passed, a quarter of an hour, and then there came to her ears the noise which had first aroused her — the shuffling of bare feet upon a hard, smooth surface. She had caught a glimpse of the passage when Dr Cody had opened the door. She knew it was covered with oilcloth, and it was on this that the feet were moving. Nearer and nearer they came, and then stopped. Somebody turned the handle of the door and drew back the bolts. She was frozen with terror; could not move, could only stand staring blankly at the door, waiting for the apparition which would be revealed to her.

Again the handle turned, but the door did not move. Whoever it was had not the key. There was a silence. Somebody was trying to break in the door, and she caught a glimpse of a huge, misshapen toe in the space between the door and the floor. Then, from under the door, came three huge, squat fingers. They were wet and red with blood. The hand gripped the bottom of the door and strove to lift it.

At the sight of that obscene hand the spell was broken, and she screamed, and, turning, fled in desperate panic to the chair beneath the skylight. As she looked up she saw a face staring down at her through the window – the white face of Cawler, the chauffeur.

20

It was more than accident that took Dick Martin to the library the previous afternoon. He had come to feel that a day without a glimpse of this tantalizing girl was a day wasted. And he remembered, with a sense of virtuous pride, that he was a subscriber and entitled to walk into this sedate establishment and demand, if he so desired, the most unintelligible volumes on biophysics.

"Miss Lansdown is gone," said one of the officials. "It is her early day. She went away with a lady."

"With her mother?" he asked.

"No," said the girl, shaking her head; "it wasn't Mrs Lansdown. I know her very well. It was a lady who drove up to the door in a Rolls. I've never seen her before."

There was nothing remarkable in this. Although she was beginning to fill a large space of his life, Dick scarcely knew the girl, and certainly knew nothing of her friends. He was disappointed, for he had intended, on the lamest excuse, to take her to tea that afternoon. He waited till nearly seven before he called at Coram Street. Here his excuse for the visit was even lamer, and he accounted this one of his unlucky days when Mrs Lansdown smilingly told him that the girl had telephoned, in her absence, to say she would not be home to dinner.

"She has a girl friend and often dines with her – probably she will go on to a theatre afterwards. Won't you stay and keep me company at dinner, Mr Martin? Though I'm afraid I'm rather an uninteresting substitute for Sybil!"

He was glad to accept the invitation, hoping that before he left, Sybil would put in an appearance; but, though he prolonged his visit to the limits of politeness, she had not returned when he took his leave at eleven o'clock. Until then he had not made any reference to the story the librarian had told him.

"Your daughter's friend is a fairly rich young lady?" he asked.

Mrs Lansdown was surprised.

"No, indeed, she works for her living; she is a cashier in a drug store."

She saw the frown gather on his face, and asked quickly: "Why?"

"Somebody called for Sybil with a car – a Rolls," he said; "somebody that the librarian did not know."

Mrs Lansdown smiled.

"That isn't very remarkable. Jane Allen isn't very rich, but she has a number of very wealthy relatives, and probably it was her aunt who called."

He lingered outside the house for a quarter of an hour, consuming three cigarettes before, a thoroughly dissatisfied man, he walked home. His uneasiness he analysed to his own discredit. He was not considering, he told himself, whether the girl was in any kind of scrape, and the real secret of his annoyance was purely personal and selfish.

His flat seemed strangely empty that night. As was his wont, he walked through all the rooms, and paid particular attention to the little kitchen balcony. Behind every door he had put a portable alarm, a tiny triangle to which was attached a bell, the apex of the triangle being fixed in the wood of the door, so that any attempt to open it would assuredly arouse him. This done, he switched the telephone through to his room, undressed slowly, and went to bed.

Sleep did not come easily, and he took a book and read. The clock was striking one as he dozed off. He was half awake and half asleep when the telephone bell sounded in the passage, and, putting on the light, he sat up and took the instrument from the table by the bed.

"Hullo!"

"Trunk call," said a man's voice.

There was a click, a silence, and then:

"*Murder... I'm being murdered. Oh, God! They are here...the boys...murder!*"

His spine crept.

"Who is it speaking?" he asked quickly.

There was no answer.

"Who are you? Where are you speaking from?"

Still no answer. Then a deep groan and a curse, a shriek that ended in a thick sob.

"Don't touch me, don't touch me. Help!"

There was a crash, and no further sound. Dick worked rapidly at the hanger of the telephone and presently got the exchange.

"Where was I called from?"

"Somewhere in Sussex," said the local man. "Do you want me to find out?"

"Yes – and quick! I'm Mr Martin, of Scotland Yard. Will you call me?"

"I'll ring you in a minute," was the reply.

Instantly Dick was out of bed and dressing with feverish haste. The voice he had not recognized, but some instinct told him that this call was no hoax and that he had listened in to the very act of slaughter. He dare not ring Sneed, in case he interfered with the call which was coming through.

He was lacing his shoes when the bell rang.

"It was from South Weald, Sussex – "

Dick uttered an oath. Cody's house! It was Cody speaking; he remembered the voice now.

"Get the nearest police station to South Weald and tell them I asked you to send men straight away to Mr Cody's place, Weald House. There is trouble there. Will you do this for me?"

And when the man had replied in the affirmative: "Now get me Brixton 9007," he said.

Sneed must know, if he could only arouse that lethargic man from his sleep. To his surprise, the call came through almost immediately, and Sneed's voice answered him.

"I've been playing bridge with a few nuts from headquarters," he began. "It was like taking money from children – "

"Listen, Sneed," said Dick urgently. "There's trouble at Cody's place. He's just called me through."

In a few words he gave the gist of the terrible message which had reached him.

"That sounds bad," said Sneed's thoughtful voice. "I've got a car down here – "

"Mine is faster. I'll pick you up. Where are you?"

"I'll be under the railway arch in Brixton Road. I can bring a couple of men with me – Inspector Elbert and Sergeant Staynes. They are here with me."

This was good news. He knew instinctively that in the work ahead of him he would need all the assistance he could procure.

"I'll be with you in ten minutes."

Dick grabbed his overcoat and flew to the door. As he flung it open he stepped back in amazement. A white-faced woman was standing on the threshold.

"Mrs Lansdown!" he gasped, and his heart sank.

"Sybil did not go with Jane Allen," she said in a low voice.

"She hasn't returned?"

Mrs Lansdown shook her head.

"Come in," said Dick, and took her into the dining-room. "Now, tell me – "

Mrs Lansdown's story was all he might have expected. She had waited until twelve, and then, growing a little uneasy, had walked round to the boarding-house where Jane Allen lived. She found the girl in bed. She had not seen Sybil, nor had she made any arrangements to meet her.

"Is there anybody else to whom she could have gone?"

"I have been able to ring up two friends she might be staying with, but they have not seen her," said Mrs Lansdown. "I was fortunate enough to get in touch with the girl who works with Sybil at the library, and she described the woman who came for my girl; a very overdressed woman of middle age, who wore a lot of jewellery and spoke in a very common voice."

Mrs Cody! She saw him turn pale and gripped him by the arm.

"Is anything very wrong?" she asked huskily.

"I don't know. Will you stay here? I'm going to see."

"Can I come with you?"

"No, no." He shook his head. "I'll be gone a little more than an hour, then I'll phone you. Won't you try to read? You will find books in my room that will interest you."

She shook her head.

"I must go home in case Sybil returns. But don't wait for me; I have a cab at the door."

There was no time for polite protests. He dashed out of the house ahead of her, and was in the mews unlocking the garage door before she had reached the cab.

Within a few minutes of the promised time the big car drew up under the railway at Brixton, where Sneed and his two friends were waiting.

Jump in," said Dick; "I've something to tell you. I'm trying to get the hang of it – your head will be cooler than mine."

As the machine sped southward he told of Sybil's disappearance.

"That was Mrs Cody all right," sneed said. "I met her some time ago. She's certainly a daisy. But what harm could she do the girl?"

Dick Martin was not prepared with an answer.

"The Sussex sleuths will be there before we reach the house – " he began, but the other scoffed.

"You don't know our police system, or you wouldn't be so sure. Probably the nearest station to South Weald hasn't a telephone; and even if it had, it's unlikely that a police officer would act on telephoned instructions unless he were sure of the sender. I'm not so certain that we aren't on a fool's chase."

"I've thought of that, too," said Martin; "but, weighing it up, there are long odds against that possibility. No, the man who phoned me was not acting."

They passed the next quarter of an hour without speaking.

"We're somewhere near Stalletti's house, aren't we?" said Sneed, waking from a doze.

"On the left," replied the other curtly.

They flashed past the dark entrance of the drive. From the road the house was invisible, and only the high trees standing against the moonlit sky marked its situation.

"Rum thing about this Lord Selford business," said Sneed meditatively. "There's trouble wherever you touch it. I wonder what he's done?"

"What who's done? Selford?" asked Dick, rousing himself with a start.

The fat man nodded.

"Why is he keeping out of England? Why is he running around like a Christianized Wandering Jew? Wearing out his shoe-leather whilst the ancestral chair is collecting dust? You've never seen him, have you?"

"No," said Dick shortly. "I've seen a photograph of him, but I've never seen him."

Sneed shifted round and peered through the darkness at his companion.

"Seen a photograph of him?" he said slowly.

"Sure," said Dick. "He was in Cape Town the day the new Governor-General arrived. He came out on to the balcony of the hotel to watch the procession, and one of the newspaper boys took a picture shot of the crowd. I didn't know this, only the hotel porter had seen it in the paper and pointed him out to me. And then I went along to the newspaper office and got a first-hand print and had it enlarged."

"What is he like?" asked Sneed curiously.

"I'll tell you one of these days," was the unsatisfactory reply, and soon after they were speeding down the secondary road and through the tiny village of South Weald.

There was no unusual stir, and at Sneed's suggestion they stopped at the little cottage where the village patrol lived and had his tiny lock-up for the infrequent offenders who came his way. The man's wife opened an upper window when they knocked.

"No, sir – the constable is out tonight. He is up at Chapley Woods looking for poachers with Sir John's gamekeeper."

"Have you a telephone?"

There was one, and she had taken a message which would be given to her husband when he arrived home in the early hours of the morning.

Dick restarted the car, and in a few minutes –

"Here we are," he said, and pulled up his car with a jerk before the gates of Weald House.

He sounded his horn, but there was no sign of light or movement in the little lodge, which, he afterwards learned, was untenanted. Getting down, he tried the gates, and found one was fastened by a slip catch. Throwing it open, he unbolted the second and, fastening both gates back, remounted his machine and went cautiously up the drive.

The bulk of the house was visible for fifty yards before they came to it. No light showed, and there was no evidence of human activity. He rang the bell and waited, listening. Again he pressed the electric push, and supplemented this by banging on the heavy panel of the door. Three minutes were lost in this way, and then Sneed sent one of his friends to throw gravel at one of the upper windows.

"There seems to be nobody up. I'll give them another few minutes," said Sneed, "and then we'll force a window."

These, he discovered on inspection, were heavily shuttered, but flanking the porch were two narrow panes of ground glass.

"You'll never get through there," said Sneed, perhaps conscious of his own bulk.

"Won't I?" said Dick grimly.

He went back to the car and returned with a screwdriver. Whilst the stout man watched admiringly, he removed the whole pane and drew it out. His one fear was that behind the glass was a shutter or bar, but apparently the narrowness of the window was regarded by Mr Cody as a sufficient protection.

Assisted by the two detectives, he slipped sideways and feet foremost through an opening, which, it seemed, no human being could pass. His head was the most difficult part of his anatomy to squeeze through, but presently he was in the hall with no damage to himself save a slight laceration to one of his ears.

The hall was in complete darkness. There came no sound but the slow, solemn ticking of a clock on a landing above. Then suddenly he sniffed. Dick Martin had an abnormal sense of smell, and now he scented something which turned him cold. Flashing his lamp on the door, he took off the chain, pulled back the bolts and admitted his companions.

"There's murder here," he said tersely "Can you smell blood?"

"Blood?" said the startled Sneed. "Good God, no! Can you?"

Martin nodded. He was searching the walls for the electric light switch, and after a while he found a board with five, and these he turned over. One lamp lit in the hall and one on the landing above, out of sight. Outside switches controlled the lights of this room. He pointed to the door. Suddenly he felt Sneed's hand grip his arm.

"Look!" muttered the inspector.

He was glaring upstairs, and, following his eyes, Dick saw something which at first he did not understand. And then slowly he realized that he was looking at the shadow of a figure cast against the wall of the landing. It was obviously leaning over the unseen banisters, for the carved uprights and the broad rail showed clearly against the papered wall. The light he had lit on the landing above was evidently placed low, and behind the motionless figure, and thus it was that the shadow was clear and without distortion.

Slipping an automatic from his pocket, he ran up the stairs sideways, looking back over his shoulder, and Sneed saw him halt on the landing, look for a moment, and then: "Come up, Sneed."

The inspector followed, reached the first landing, and turned to look into a white face that was staring down at him with unseeing eyes – the face of a stout woman who was half leaning, half lying, across the banisters, both her hands clenched, and on her face a look of unimaginable horror.

21

"Dead," said Sneed, unnecessarily, as they went slowly up the five stairs that brought them to the top landing.

There was no sign of violence, and they now saw what kept the body erect. She had been kneeling on a low settee which ran flush with the banisters, and by the accident of balance, when death had come, had retained her position. Reverently they lowered the body to the ground, whilst the inspector conducted a brief examination.

"Fright," he said briefly. "I saw a man like this about ten years ago. She saw something – horrible!"

"Has she got anything in her hand?" asked Dick suddenly, and prised open the tightly clenched fingers.

As he did so something fell to the parquet floor with a clang, and he uttered an exclamation of amazement.

It was a key – the fellow to those which reposed at his bankers.

The two men looked at one another without a word. Then: "Where is Cody?" asked Sneed.

He was searching the wall for the telephone wiring, which he had expected to see, and, guessing his thoughts, Dick Martin pointed downstairs.

"You're looking for the phone? It is in the library; I saw it when I was here the other night. Moses! Look at that!"

The stairs were carpeted with dark grey carpet, thick and luxurious to the tread, and he was gaping at something he had not seen when he came up the stairs with the light in his face – the red print of a bare foot! Stooping, he touched it with his finger.

"Blood," he said. "I thought I smelt it! I wonder where those feet picked up that stuff?"

They found the imprint again lower down. In fact, on every second step the stain lay, and the nearer they got to the bottom of the stairs the more sharply defined it was.

"He came up two steps at a time – three here," nodded Dick. "We'll probably find the trail in the hall."

The vestibule was floored with polished wood, but there were three or four Persian rugs of a dark colour, and the prints on these had escaped their notice until they began to search for them.

"Here is one," said Dick, "and here is another." He pointed. "They lead from that room. Bare feet must have wandered aimlessly here – the footmarks are on every rug."

He tried the handle of the door, but it did not move.

"A spring lock," explained Sneed; "fastens automatically when it's closed. What is in the room opposite?"

Facing the closed door was another, which was unfastened. Two series of lights were burning, which at first aroused Dick's suspicion, until he remembered that he himself had turned them on from the switches in the hall. It was evidently a dining-room, beautifully furnished, and empty. The windows were shuttered; there was no sign of anything unusual, and he returned to the problem of the locked door.

He carried a very comprehensive range of tools in the "boot" of his machine; but it was the jack he used for raising his car when he replaced a wheel that made the opening of the door possible. The small crowbar he tried to insert between door and lintel was useless, but when he used the jack, improvising a brace with the long hall table, the lock burst.

As the door flew open, he caught a glimpse of the library where he had been received by Cody, and his eyes, focussing on the writing-table, where the little red lamp still burnt, saw instantly the overturned telephone. He took two steps into the room, followed by Sneed, when the lights went out, not only in the room but in the hall.

"Anybody touch the switch?"

"No, sir," said the detective outside the door.

Dick lugged out his electric lamp, which he had replaced as soon as he had found the switchboard, and walked gingerly towards the desk. Coming round the end of a large settee which ran across the room, he saw the huddled figure lying by the side of the desk, and it only needed a glance to tell him all that he feared.

Bertram Cody lay on his back with his legs doubled sideways, and he was not a pleasant sight; for the man who killed him had used no other weapon than the bent and bloodstained poker by his side. His hand still gripped the receiver of the telephone, and he had evidently been in the act of talking when the last and fatal blow was struck.

All the drawers of the desk had been turned out, emptied, and their contents apparently taken away, for not so much as a sheet of paper had been left behind by the murderer.

Sneed pulled a pair of white cotton gloves from his pocket, drew them on, and, carefully lifting the poker, laid it on the desk. He gave his instructions in a low tone to one of his men, who went out of the library, evidently to the telephone connection which they had seen in the dining-room, for Dick heard him talking.

"I've sent for the Scotland Yard photographer and the local police," he said. "There are probably finger-prints on the poker that will be very useful."

There was a door at the farther end of the room, and this, Dick discovered, was ajar. It opened upon a small apartment which was probably used as a breakfast-room, for on the small buffet there was a hot plate and an electric toaster. Here one of the windows was open.

"It was Cody who phoned, of course," said Dick, pulling his lip thoughtfully; "and Mrs Cody who brought Sybil Lansdown here. Sneed, we've got to find that girl!"

He was sick with fear, and the elder man could not guess what agony of doubt lay behind the calmness of his manner.

"Whoever did this is somewhere around," said Sneed. "The lights did not go off by accident."

At that moment the man he had sent into the dining-room to telephone to the Yard came back.

"The phone wire was cut while I was talking," he announced, and there was a silence.

"Are you sure?"

"Absolutely certain, sir," said the detective, "I had just got through to the Yard and was talking to Mr Elmer when the instrument went dead."

Two of the three Scotland Yard men carried torches, fortunately, and one of them went to find the fuse-box, and came back to announce that there was no sign of a blow-out.

"I'll explore upstairs," said Dick. "You hang on here, Sneed."

He went up the stairs, past the dreadful figure lying on the landing, and walked from room to room. Here there was neither sign of disorder nor evidence that the girl was in the house. And then, as he turned his lamp on the dark carpet, he saw the stains again and trailed them. The barefooted man had evidently wandered up and down the corridor, and it was clear to Dick Martin that he was wounded, for whilst the footprints were no longer visible, little spots of blood showed at intervals, and there was a smear against the white wall which almost located the position of the wound.

Soon after he found a little bundle of grimy rags, which undoubtedly had been used as a bandage. The solution came to him in a moment. The killer was the man he had winged in Selford Park – the half-nude savage who had attacked him that night at Gallows Hill. His murderous exertions had displaced the bandage and the wound had begun to bleed again.

He followed the track until it turned into the beginning of a narrow flight of stairs leading to the storey above. He was now on the attic floor, and evidently there were two ways to this floor, for only three rooms opened from the passage in which he found himself. The first was a lumber room; the second was an apartment which held nothing more sinister than a large zinc cistern. It was in the third and last room on the left that he made his discovery. A panel of the door, which hung upon one hinge, was broken; the lock had been smashed into three pieces. As the beam of his lamp went systematically round the room he saw a bed, and then his heart missed a beat. On the floor, almost at his feet, was a little handkerchief, dappled red.

He picked it up with a shaking hand and saw the embroidered initials "S L". Sybil's!

22

Sneed came up at his call, and together the men searched the room.

"Bloodstains on that door; did you notice them? Down there at the bottom," said Sneed, working his lamp along the panel. "Finger-prints, and pretty distinct! Whoever it was, he put his hand under the door and tried to lift it off its hinge – look at the size of the prints! This was the gentleman who visited you, Martin!"

Dick nodded.

"No other signs of violence. No blood on the floor," mused Sneed, and stared up at the open skylight. "I'm too fat to go up there. See what you can find."

There was a chair underneath the square aperture, and Dick, springing on to it, caught the edge of the skylight and drew himself up. He was on a level ledge of roof about three feet wide. A low parapet ran its full length on the one side, whilst on the other the roof rose steeply to the ridge pole. Dick sent his light ahead of him and saw two yellow projections overtopping the parapet.

"A builder's ladder," he said, and made his way towards it.

It was easy to see why the ladder had escaped attention when he made his first superficial survey of the house. At this point the outside wall of the house was thrown back at a right angle, and it was in this angle that the ladder had been planted, none too securely.

"She must have had some sort of outside help," he said, returning to his companion to report his find. "It couldn't have been the servants, because there are no servants in the house."

"Help me up," said the inspector.

It seemed almost impossible to lift that huge man through the skylight, but in truth he was as strong as an ox, and to Dick's relief the only assistance he needed was approval of his agility.

"What about friend Cawler?" suggested Sneed, breathing noisily.

He was peering down at the leaden roof, and suddenly: "Here are your blood spots," he said, "and here they are again on the ladder. That smear is distinct enough."

Dick Martin turned cold with dread, and the hope that had suddenly revived in his heart vanished.

"I'll hold the ladder; get down and see what you can find," said Sneed, and braced himself against the parapet, gripping the top supports, while Dick descended to the dark ground, stopping now and again to examine the supports.

He found himself in what was evidently the beginning of a kitchen garden. It was hopeless to look for traces of feet upon the gravelled pathway, which followed a straight course through beds of growing vegetables to a small orchard.

"Hold the ladder," shouted Sneed; "I'll come down."

In spite of his anxiety, Martin could not repress a smile at the courage of the big man. He gripped the ladder whilst Sneed came down with a surprising agility, and together they made a brief reconnaissance of the ground.

"They couldn't have gone towards the house because that hedge shuts it off. There is only one exit, and that is through the orchard." Inspector Sneed scratched his head in perplexity. "We can't do any harm following the path to its end."

They had passed the first vegetable bed and had reached the beginning of the second.

"I think it wouldn't be a bad idea – " began Sneed.

Bang! Bang!

From the darkness ahead of them leapt two pencils of flame; something whizzed past them with the noise of an angry wasp.

"Lights out and lie down," hissed the stout inspector, and in the fraction of a second they were lying side by side on the path.

And then, from ahead of them, broke a furious staccato fusillade of fire. The whine of the bullets seemed continuous. The smack and rustle of them as they passed through the foliage or struck against some solid billet was almost continuous. As suddenly as the shooting began, it ceased. The two men listened intently. There was no sound, until there came to Dick's ears a faint "swish! swish!" as if the coat of their unknown assailant was brushing the edge of a bush. The pistol he held in his hand stiffly before him spat twice in the direction whence the noise had come. There was no other indication of human presence, no cry or proof of accelerated movement.

"What have they got there?" whispered Sneed, who was breathing heavily. "A regiment of soldiers or something?"

"One man with two automatic pistols," was the answer in the same tone. "I couldn't count 'em, but I guess twenty shots were fired."

A few more minutes passed, and then: "We can get up now, I think."

"I think not," said Dick.

Dick was already crawling forward on his hands and knees. It was a painful proceeding; his neck ached, the sharp gravel cut through the knees of his trousers, and his knuckles were bleeding – for it is not easy to crawl with a large-calibre automatic in one's hand. In this fashion he came to the place where the gravel path ended and the earth track between the trees began.

He listened for a long time, then stood up.

"It's all right," he said.

Hardly were the words out of his mouth when a pistol exploded almost in his face.

23

The wind of the bullet came so close to his left eye that it almost blinded him momentarily. He was stunned with the proximity of the explosion, staggered, and dropped to his knees, and then, ahead of him, he heard the sound of running feet, and, scrambling up, he darted forward, only to fall headlong again; for the assassin had fixed a trip wire between two of the trees, and later they were to find that this cover to retreat had been installed at intervals along the path. Death had been very near to Dick Martin that night.

"Could he have got away?"

Dick nodded.

"Yes," he said shortly. "There is a side road runs parallel with the orchard for about two hundred yards; I made a fairly thorough examination of the house before my first visit. I particularly wanted to know the lay-out of the grounds in case there was trouble, and I took the precaution of examining a plan of the estate before I left town."

He went back to the house, baffled and fretful. Where was Sybil Lansdown? He told himself a dozen times that the girl could be in no immediate danger without his knowing. Why he should know he could not for the life of him tell; but he was satisfied in his mind that his instinct was not leading him into error. When they reached the house, all the lights were burning and one of the officers had a report to make. There was, he said, an outside transformer; a steel box on the farther side of the lawn, and the iron door of this was found to be open.

"That is where the current was disconnected," he explained. "The telephone wire was easy; it was cut outside the house."

With the aid of the lights they were able to make a very complete examination of the house, but there was no clue of any kind, and whilst they were inspecting Mrs Cody's bedroom the local police arrived. Apparently Scotland Yard had heard enough of the interrupted conversation, before the wire was cut, to communicate with the Sussex police, and a special force of detectives had been packed off from Chichester by car.

Sneed waited until the officers had distributed themselves through the house, and went on with the work which their arrival had interrupted. He was trying a bunch of keys on a small box of Indian workmanship.

"Found this under the bed," he said laconically. "Queer how a certain class of people keep things under their beds, and another class keep 'em under their pillows. That fits, I think."

He turned the key and opened the box. It was filled with papers – letters, old bills, a concert programme of a very remote date, and possibly associated, in the mind of the poor dead woman, with what there was of romance in life.

"You take the top bundle; I'll search the rest."

Dick untied the ribbon which fastened the papers together and began to read. There was a letter or two written in childish handwriting, and one scrawled note signed "Your loving nefew, JOHN CAWLER."

"I thought she only had one nephew – Tom?"

"You never know how many nephews people have," said the indifferent Sneed.

"But this speaks about John. It must be his brother?"

Sneed looked up.

"I wonder where that darned chauffeur is? I sent a call out to pull him in. He's been missing since last night, and I don't exclude the possibility of his having had something to do with this murder."

"I rule that out entirely," said Dick promptly. "I know Cawler; he's not that kind of man. I wouldn't trust him with any goods valuable and portable, but the habitual criminal is not a murderer."

Sneed grunted a half agreement, and went on reading. Presently, almost at the bottom of the bundle Dick had under examination, he found a note written in a clerkly hand.

"Dear Mrs Cawler (it ran),
"I have just seen Stalletti, and he tells me that his lordship is very ill indeed. I wish you would send me the latest news, for reasons which you well know and which need not be mentioned.
"Yours faithfully,
"H BERTRAM."

"He calls himself Bertram – but the handwriting is Cody's," said Sneed, puzzled. "Bertram? I seem to know the name."

Dick was looking past the letter into vacancy.

"Then they were all acquainted," he said slowly. "Cody, Mrs Cody, Stalletti, and the late Lord Selford. When Cody said he knew nothing of the Selfords he was lying."

"You knew that anyway," said the other.

Dick turned over letter after letter, but no further information reached him except a copy of a marriage certificate. This, however, he did not find till the box had been completely turned out.

"Humph!" he said. "They married about eight months after the late Lord Selford's death, by special licence. Stalletti was a witness, and William Brown. Now, who the devil is William Brown?"

"It's not an uncommon name," said Mr Sneed sententiously.

Their search finished, they went back to the library. Sneed took the hollow-eyed young man by the arm and led him to a quiet corner.

"Where do we go from here?" he asked.

"I don't know," said the other helplessly.

He put his hand in his pocket, took out the key and examined it.

"Number three! I've got four more to find, and then somebody will be hanged for this night's work!"

"Where shall we go from here?" asked Sneed again.

Dick looked at his watch. The hands pointed to a quarter-past two.

"Selford Manor," he said briefly. "It has just occurred to me that we're only three miles away from that home of the nobility."

They went out into the open, where Dick had left his car.

"What do you expect to find there?"

"I'm not sure yet," said Dick, as he got into the seat and put his foot on the starter. "But I have an idea that I shall find – something!"

The car moved, but not steadily. It waddled and jarred forward a few paces, and then Dick stopped and jumped out.

"I'm afraid I shall have to go on my two big feet," he said, and turned the light on to the wheels.

Every tyre had been slashed in a dozen places and was quite flat.

24

That moment of terror when Sybil stared up into the round face of Cawler, the chauffeur, remained with her all her life. Behind she heard the grunts and thuds of the beast-man who was trying to open the door. Above her, behind the bars and the glass, another possible enemy. The face disappeared for a moment, and then she heard the sound of hideous squeaking and the grating was turned back on its rusty hinge. A few seconds and the frame of the skylight was lifted, and a hand reached down to her. Without a moment's hesitation she sprang on to the chair, gripped the hand, and found herself being pulled upward.

"Hold on to the edge for a minute – I'm puffed!" gasped Cawler, and she obeyed.

Over her shoulder she saw the door bulging, and then there came a crash as a huge body was thrown against it.

"Up with you!" said the chauffeur, and, stretching down, gripped her beneath the arms and pulled her far enough up to enable her, by her own exertions, to reach the flat, lead-covered roof.

Cawler looked round anxiously. As he gazed at the door he saw a panel shiver. Holding the girl by the arm he drew her along the roof. An old lantern, illuminated by a candle, was all the light there was to guide them, but she saw the end of the ladder, and, without a word of instruction, swung herself over and, remembering a trick of her childhood, slid down; it was not dignified, but it was rapid. She had hardly reached the ground before she was joined by Cawler.

He looked back anxiously at the parapet. The moon was momentarily obscured by clouds, but there was enough light to see the silhouette of the giant man as he too came to the ladder. There was no time to pull it down. Gripping the girl by the arm, they raced along a path, turned abruptly, and, threading their way through the trees, ran without stopping until they reached a shallow ditch, across which he assisted her.

Cawler had tossed the lantern away before the flight began. They had no other light to aid them but the fitful rays of the moon. At the other side of the ditch he stopped.

"Don't make a noise," he whispered.

She could hear nothing, but he seemed uncertain.

"If I could only get at my car," he muttered. "Come on!"

They laboured through a field of growing corn until they came to a gate, which was open. Now they were on a road and facing a very high, old wall.

"That's Selford Park," explained Cawler, and the girl started.

Selford Park! She had no idea they were anywhere near that dreadful place, and she shivered.

"There's a gap in the wall farther along; I think that'll be the best place to take you. If he gets on our track we shan't be able to shake him off."

"Who is he?" she asked, and then: "What happened? I heard somebody scream."

"So did I," said Cawler in a low voice. "I thought it was you. That's why I got the ladder and came up to see what was happening. I've been up there before, and I know that old skylight like a book."

He did not explain that he was by nature curious and suspicious, and that he had his own views as to Cody's sincerity in certain matters and had indulged in a little private investigation of his own. As it happened, his theory that Cody was a swell mobsman (Mr Cawler invariably theorized on a magnificent scale) was miles away from the truth; but he had made many surreptitious visits into the forbidden portions of the house without succeeding, however, in confirming his natural prejudices against the man who was his master.

"Something's happening; I know that," he said, as they walked along the road. "I've seen him once before – that naked man. At least, he's not naked; he's got an old pair of breeches on, but he don't wear any shirt."

"Who is he?" she asked, in a horrified whisper.

"I don't know. A sort of giant – a bit mad, I think. I only saw him at a distance once, and he scared the life out of me. I've got an idea – but that won't interest you. Here's the hole in the wall."

It was not visible, even in daylight, for the gap was filled with a seemingly impassable barrier of rhododendrons, but Mr Cawler had evidently been here before also, for he lifted a bough, and, crawling under, she found herself inside the park.

It was not that portion of the park with which she was familiar, and he told her, as they trudged across the billowy grass, that it was called Shepherds' Meadows, and that here the old lord had kept his famous Southdowns.

He kept up an intermittent flow of talk; told her, to her surprise, that Mrs Cody was his aunt.

"She brought me up when I was a kid, me and my brother Johnny; he died when I was about six."

"Have you been with her all your life?" asked the girl, glad to have some interest to take her mind off her experience.

He laughed contemptuously.

"With her? Lord, no! I got away as soon as I could."

"Wasn't she kind to you?"

"She's never heard the word," was the uncompromising reply. "Kind? I'd say she was! If I went to bed without feeling hungry I used to think I was ill! She used to whack me to keep her in good shape, the same as you take dumb-bell exercise. She hated Johnny worse than me. He was my twin brother. I reckon he was pretty lucky to die."

She listened in amazement.

"And yet you went back to her?"

Cawler did not immediately answer, and when he did he prefaced his words with a little chuckle.

"She made good and I made bad," he said. "Not to tell you a lie, miss, I've been in prison sixteen times, mainly for hooking."

"For thieving?" she guessed.

"That's right," he said, in no sense abashed. "I'm a natural-born thief. Motor-cars mostly. I've taken more cars from race-tracks than you'll ever own, young lady. But the last time I was up before the judge," he added in a more serious tone, "he gave me a warning that the next time I went up to the Old Bailey I'd be charged as an 'habitual'. That means a man who's always doing the same kind of crime, and they can always give you twelve years for that, so I quit. Came down on dear auntie for a job. I don't know why she took me on. Perhaps she thought, being a relation, I'd do any dirty work she wanted done – and I've done one or two queer jobs."

He stopped and motioned her to be silent, and suddenly lying down looked along the fairly level patch of ground across which they were moving. The landscape was unfamiliar to her. On their left was what looked like a high white cliff, and she saw at its foot the gleam of water.

"That's the quarry," he said, following the direction of her eyes. "There is a sort of road running along the top, but it is very dangerous – no rails or wall or anything. People have been killed falling over."

He stopped again and looked back the way they had come. Evidently he saw something.

"You go on," he whispered. "Bear to the left. There's a bit of a wood there. Keep well away from the quarry."

"Who is it you see?" she asked, her knees trembling.

"I don't know." He was deliberately evasive. "You walk on and do as I tell you, and don't make too much noise."

She was terrified at the idea of being alone, but his instructions were so urgent that she could not refuse, and, turning, she made in the direction of the little copse which she saw outlined against the sky.

Cawler waited, flat on his face, his eyes watching the figure that was aimlessly wandering left and right, but coming inevitably in his direction. Fear, as we understand fear, Mr Cawler did not know. His shrewd Cockney wit, allied to a certain ruthlessness in combat, steeled him for the coming encounter. In his hand he gripped a long, steel, flat spanner, the only weapon he had brought with him, and as the great awkward figure loomed up before him, Tom Cawler leapt at him.

The sound of an animal howl of rage, the thud and flurry of battle came to the ears of the fearful girl, and she ran forward blindly. In the dark she stumbled into a tree and dropped, breathless, to the ground; but with a superhuman effort she scrambled to her feet and continued her flight, feeling her way through the closely grown copse. Every minute seemed to bring her to some new impenetrable barrier which defied circumvention.

Now she was clear of the wood and crossing a level stretch of grassland. Again she was climbing. No sound came from behind her. She was ignorant of the direction she was taking, or whither this erratic path of hers would lead; and when she came to another wood, she thought that she had run in a circle and returned to the place whence she had started. And then, most unexpectedly, she came into a clearing. The moonlight showed the white dome of a rock, and threw into shadow the black gap in its face. She nearly fainted. She was at the mouth of the Selford tombs, and the iron gate was open!

Her heart thumped painfully. It required the exercise of a supreme will to prevent herself from collapsing. Presently, gritting her teeth and commanding her faltering limbs, she walked towards the mouth of the tomb. The key was in the lock, she saw, and peered fearfully down into its dark depths. As she hesitated, she heard something behind her – a deep, sobbing, blubbering sound that froze her blood.

That beast-shape was coming through the wood after her. She reeled against the face of the tomb, her hands gripping the bars of the open gate, and then, with a sudden resolve, half-hysterical with terror, she darted into the mouth of the vault, and, slamming the gate behind her, thrust her hand through the bars, turned the key, and withdrew it.

She listened; there was silence in the tomb, and, creeping down the moss-grown stairs, she reached the first chamber. At the foot of the stairs she waited, listening, and after a while she heard the soft pad of feet above and a sound of crying. She shrank back towards the barred gate which separated the antechamber from the tomb. And then a shadow fell athwart the upper door, and she breathed painfully, her eyes fixed on the steps. Suppose he broke the lock? And she was alone…down here with the dead, in the dark.

She pushed her hand through the bars, and even as she wondered and dreaded, a new horror afflicted her; for her hand was suddenly gripped by a large, cold, clammy paw that had reached out from the darkness of the tomb.

With a scream she turned to face the new terror.

25

She could see nothing. Fighting like a tiger to free herself, her other hand passed through the bars and caught a wild tangle of beard.

"Hush!" The voice was deep, sepulchral. "I will not harm you if you tell me what you do here."

It was human, at any rate, more human than the thing that had been chasing her.

"I am Sybil – Lansdown," she gasped. "I came down here to get away from – a horrible – "

"So!" The grip on her wrist relaxed. "I will open the door. Stand back, if you please; do not move until I have lit the lamp."

The door was opened and she nearly fell through.

She saw a flicker of flame, heard a glass globe tinkle. He had lit a small kerosene lamp, which cast an eerie light upon the weird scene. She looked at the man curiously. His sallow, lined face; his long black beard, which, with a woman's intuition, she knew was dyed; his unsavoury frock-coat, splashed and stained till its original colour could only be guessed at; the little black skull cap on the back of his head – all these combined to give him a peculiarly sinister appearance.

In front of the door with seven locks was a small leather hold-all, which was open, revealing a number of instruments. One, resembling a gimlet, she saw, being inserted in the second lock of the door.

"What frightened you, my little one?" His black eyes were fixed on hers, and seemed to possess an hypnotic quality, for she could not remove her gaze.

"A – a man," she stammered.

He lit a cigarette very slowly – indeed with something of a ritual – and blew a cloud of smoke to the vaulted ceiling.

"At three o'clock in the morning?" He arched his eyebrows. "Surely the young miss who wanders about the country in the middle of the night is not to be frightened by a man? Sit down – on the floor. You are too tall for me, Women who are taller than me dominate, and I cannot suffer domination."

He took the gimlet shape from the door, replaced it in the tool kit, and rolled up the leather, strapping it very carefully and deliberately.

"You have come to spy on me – yes? I heard you close the gate and creep down the stairs – I am in a quandary! What am I to do with a young lady who spies upon me? You realize, of course, that I am seriously compromised and that, if I tell you I am an antiquarian and interested in these strange and ancient mysteries, you will laugh in your sleeve and not believe me, nor will your employers. What was your name?"

She had to wet her dry lips before she replied. She saw his eyes narrow.

"Sybil Lansdown?" he said, almost sharply. "You are, of course, the girl – how coincident!"

He had a queer, un-English way of framing his sentences, which alone betrayed his foreign origin, for otherwise his English was perfect.

She had obeyed his command and was sitting on the stone-flagged floor.

She had never thought of hesitating or even questioning his commands, and it did not seem strange to her that she should accept his orders without any attempt to resist his wishes.

"The whole proceedings are incredibly bizarre," he said, and then for a moment turned from her to examine the door with the seven locks. His long, uncleanly fingers touched the skull's head caressingly.

"You are beyond change – she is also beyond change, for she is an old woman by an inflexible standard. Too old, too old, alas! too old!" He shook his head mournfully and again turned his dark eyes upon her. "If you were eight or nine it would be simple. But you are — what?"

"Twenty-two," she said, and his lips clicked impatiently.

"Nothing can be done except—" His eyes strayed along the narrow, cell-like doors, behind which the dead and forgotten Selfords lay in their niches, and cold fear gripped her heart with icy fingers. "You are a woman, but to me women are that!" He snapped his fingers. "They are weak material for experiment. They do not react normally — sometimes they die, and years of experiment go for nothing."

She saw him purse his wet lips thoughtfully, as he walked past her and tried one of the heavy oaken doors, peering through the rusty grating.

"The whole situation is incredibly bizarre and embarrassing — the man you saw outside, was he extraordinary of appearance?"

She nodded dumbly.

"That, of course, would be a way," he said, as if he were speaking to himself. "On the other hand, he is so clumsy — which is natural. They cannot altogether be trained out of clumsiness, because fineness of execution requires delicate mental adjustments. Could a locomotive thread a needle? No! How much easier would it be for a sewing-machine to pull a train?"

He fumbled in the pocket of his waistcoat, which scarcely met over his trousers, failed to find what he wanted, and dived his hand into the breast pocket of his frock-coat.

"Ah! Here she is!"

It was a small green phial he held in his hand, and when he shook it she heard the rattle of tablets, as she guessed. He drew the cork from the neck of the phial with his teeth and shook two little red pellets on to his hand.

"Swallow these," he said.

She held out her palm obediently.

"Incredibly bizarre and unfortunate," muttered Stalletti, as he went to the second of the tomb doors and pushed a key in the lock. "If all the doors in this miserable house opened so readily, what unhappiness and trouble would be saved, eh?"

He looked at her sharply.

"You have not done as I told you," he said.

She was sitting, the two red pellets, like evil eyes, gleaming up from the white palm.

"Quick – do not hesitate!" he said commandingly.

She raised her hand to her lips. Yet her ego was fighting subconsciously and individually against the mastery of this strange man. Obedient to an order which she did not initiate, the white teeth caught the pellets and held them. Satisfied, Mr Stalletti addressed himself to opening the third tomb. And the very physical movement of him for a second released her from his mental tyranny. The pellets dropped back into her hand.

He pulled open the wooden door, creaking and groaning, and, coming back, picked up the lamp, and giving her only a casual glance as he passed, disappeared through the door. At that second his spell was broken. She sprang to her feet and fled along the passage, slamming the grille behind her. In another second she was in the open air. One fear for the moment had slain the other, and she did not pause to look left or right for the shape that lurked outside, but flew like the wind along the path which was by now as familiar as though she had trod it all her life.

Where was Cawler? She thought of him now, but only for a second. Beyond this valley, she thought, there was another field of grass, then the wall of a farmhouse, then Selford Manor. A caretaker was there; perhaps other servants of whose existence she did not know. She remembered the last time she had come across this shallow valley. Dick Martin had been with her. At the thought of him she winced. What would she not give to have this calm personality at her elbow now!

It was still dark, but in the east the pallor of coming day had tinted the skies. Let daylight come quickly, she prayed. Another hour of tension and she would go mad.

As she crossed the farmyard she heard the rattle of a chain, and a dog strained at her with a savage yelp. But so far from this unexpected incident increasing her terror, it brought almost a sense of comfort, and she stopped, whistled, and called him by a name. There never was a dog that could scare Sybil Lansdown. She went fearlessly towards the yelping beast, and in a minute the big retriever was rubbing himself against her knee and quivering under her caressing hand.

As she stooped to release the chain that fastened him, she felt a piece of rope on the ground, and she found it was about six feet long, evidently a disused clothes-line. This would make a capital leash, and she slipped the end through the D of the dog's collar and went on her way at a slower pace and happier than she had been these twelve hours past.

By this approach she came to Selford Manor from the wings, and had to turn abruptly to the right before she was at the front of the house. Selford Manor presented an unbroken front save for its porticoed entrance, of long, narrow, and rather ugly windows. It had been partly rebuilt in the reign of Queen Anne, and its architect, by some unhappy trick of fancy, had produced all that was least lovely of that period. A narrow flower-bed ran under the windows, and a broad stone path ran parallel with its façade. Along this she walked and she did not attempt to move noiselessly. Suddenly she heard the dog growl and felt the leash grow taut. She stopped and looked round, but there was nothing suspicious in sight. It might have been a fox, she thought, slipping from one of the bush clumps which dotted the park, but he was pointing straight ahead.

Until now the windows had been blank and lifeless, but a few paces on she saw a gleam of light, and moved on tiptoe towards the window, which was the third from the entrance door. She looked into a room panelled from ceiling to floor. A candle burnt on the big oak table, which was its principal, indeed, its only, article of furniture. At first she saw nothing, and then a movement near the wide, open fireplace caught her eye, and only in time did she check the scream which rose to her lips.

A man was coming out of the shadow of the fireplace; a big lion-headed man, with a long yellow beard, and hair that fell in waves over his shoulders. He wore a pair of ragged canvas shorts that hardly reached to his bare knees, but for the rest the body was bare. The muscles rippled under the fair skin, they stood up in his arms like huge ropes; she looked, and for some queer reason was not afraid. Unaware that he was observed, the strange creature crept stealthily from his place of concealment, and, taking up the candle in his thin hand, blew it out. In that moment she had a glimpse of the vacant face and the wide, staring blue eyes that gazed unseeingly into space. She held the dog tight by the muzzle to prevent his betraying her presence, and, turning, went back the way she had come, until she reached the edge of the farmyard. Should she arouse the caretaker, or should she go on to the nearest village, taking the dog with her for protection?

She felt the cord in her hand tighten, and, with a savage snarl, the retriever leapt at something she could not see. And then she heard the sound of footsteps coming from the direction of the drive, and she found her voice at last.

"Who is there?" she demanded huskily. "Don't come any nearer."

"Thank God!" said a voice, and she nearly swooned with relief, for the man who came out of the night was Dick Martin.

26

It seemed to Captain Sneed that there was little excuse for his sometime subordinate taking the girl in his arms unless he was properly engaged to her; for Mr Sneed was a stickler for the proprieties, and though during his life he had appeared a score of times in the rôle of rescuer, he had never felt it necessary either to embrace (he called it "cuddle" vulgarly) or to hold the hand of the rescued.

"Don't tell me now," said Dick. "We'll get you some food. Poor child. You must be famished!"

"Wait!"

His hand was gripping the long steel bell-pull when she caught it.

"There's somebody in there," she said rapidly and almost incoherently. "A strange man. I saw him through the window."

Disjointedly she described what she had seen, and he did not betray his concern.

"Some tramp," he suggested when she had finished. "Were any of the windows open?"

She shook her head. She was disappointed that he took her news so calmly.

"No, I haven't seen an open window."

"It may be a friend of the caretaker's," said Dick, and pulled the bell.

The hollow clang came back to him faintly.

"Anybody asleep in the house will hear that." His arm was about the girl. She was still trembling violently and was on the verge of a breakdown, he guessed. His hand was raised to ring again when he heard a sound of feet in the stone hall and a voice demanded: "Who is there?"

"Mr Martin and Miss Lansdown," said Dick, recognizing the caretaker's voice.

Chains rattled, a lock was turned, and the door opened. The caretaker was dressed in his shirt and trousers, and had evidently come straight from his bed. He blinked owlishly at the party and asked the time.

"Come in, sir," he said. "Is anything wrong?"

"Have you any friends staying with you?" asked Dick the moment he was inside the door.

"Me, sir?" said the man in surprise. "No," and with unconscious humour, "only my wife. And you'd hardly call her a friend."

"Any man, I mean."

"No, sir," said the caretaker. "Wait a minute; I'll get a light."

Selford Manor was illuminated by an old-fashioned system of acetylene lamps, and the caretaker turned on a burner, emitting a whiff of that evil-smelling gas, before he lit a jet that illuminated the hall very effectively.

The detective's first thought was of the room in which the girl had seen the stranger, and this he entered, but when the lights were lit there was no sign of any bearded man, and as this door was the only exit and had been locked and bolted on the outside, his first thought was that the over-wrought girl had imagined the incident. But an examination of the wide chimney-place caused him to change his mind. Leaning against the brick wall of the fire recess, he found an old ash-plant walking-stick, its knob glossy with use.

"Is this yours?"

The caretaker shook his head.

"No, sir; and it wasn't there last night. I swept up this room before I went to bed. I do one room a week, and I've been rather busy today in the garden and hadn't time until after tea."

"I suppose this house is full of secret passages?" asked Dick ironically. He had a detective's proper contempt for these inventions of romantic novelists.

To his surprise the man replied in the affirmative.

"There's a Jesuit room somewhere in the house, according to all I've heard," he said. "I've never seen it myself – the old housekeeper told me about it, but I don't think she'd seen it either."

Dick went along the walls, tapping each panel, but they seemed solid enough. He threw the light of his lamp up the chimney. It was fairly narrow, considering the age of the house, and there were iron rungs placed at intervals, up which the chimney-sweeps of old times had climbed to perform their duties. He examined the wall of the fireplace carefully; there was no sign of recent scratching, and it seemed impossible that the intruder could have escaped in that direction. Carrying the stick to the light, he examined the ferrule; there was earth on it, new and moist.

"What do you make of it?" asked Sneed.

Dick was scowling at the fireplace.

"I'm blest if I know what to make of it."

He was anxious to be alone with the girl, to hear from her the story of her escape, and, cutting short his investigations, he took her into the room in which they had been received on their first night and settled her before the fire which the caretaker had lighted.

Although the night was by no means chilly, Sybil was cold and shivering, and he saw that she was nearer to collapse than he had at first supposed. Not until the caretaker came back from the kitchen with a steaming bowl of coffee and toasted bread did he attempt to question her about the night's adventures. She ate and drank ravenously, for now she realized that she had eaten nothing since the previous day's luncheon.

The two men, sitting one on each side of her on the settee, which had been pulled up to the fire, listened without comment until she had finished her story. Only once did Dick interrupt, and that was to ask her a question about the red pellets. She had thrown them away in her flight, however.

"That doesn't matter. We shall find the bottle when we take Stalletti," said Sneed impatiently. "Go on, Miss Lansdown."

At last she finished.

"It sounds to you like the ravings of a madwoman," she said ruefully. "I don't know why Mr Cody kept me. Did anything happen to him?" she asked quickly.

Dick did not answer at once.

"I heard somebody scream — it was terrible!" She shuddered. "Was it anything to do with Mr Cody?"

"Possibly." Dick evaded the question. "You say that Cawler is still in the park? You saw somebody following you — did you hear any sound of a struggle?"

She nodded, and he walked to the window and pulled back the curtains. The dawn was here, and to search the grounds would be a simple matter in daylight.

As he looked, two bright lights came into view. It was a motor-car coming up the long drive.

"Did you send for more police?" he asked Sneed over his shoulder.

"No," said Sneed in surprise. "There is no phone attached to this old-fashioned mansion, and I could not have sent if I wanted. Seems to me I know the sound of that flivver."

They walked out to the portico as the dust-covered car came to a standstill before the door and Mr Havelock jumped out.

"Is everything all right?" he asked anxiously. "Is Miss Lansdown here?"

"Yes; how did you know?"

"Is she safe?" insisted the lawyer.

"Quite safe. Come in." Dick was mystified, as the tall man followed him into the hall. "Why did you come?" he asked.

For answer, Havelock searched his waistcoat pocket, and taking out a folded sheet of paper, handed it to the detective. It was a letter bearing the embossed crest of the Ritz-Carlton, and was written in a hand with which he was, by now, familiar.

"Dear Havelock,

"I cannot explain all I have to tell in this letter. But I beg of you to go immediately to Selford Manor. Somewhere in the neighbourhood is my cousin, Sybil Lansdown, and she is in deadly peril. So is everybody associated with her – so also are you. For God's sake get the girl to the house and keep her there until I arrive. I cannot possibly get to you until the early hours of tomorrow morning. Again I implore you not to allow Miss Lansdown or her friends to leave Selford Park until I arrive.

"SELFORD."

"My front door bell rang about one o'clock in the morning, and rang so persistently that I got out of bed to discover who was the caller. I found this in my letter-box, but no messenger. At first I thought it was a hoax, and I was going back to bed when Selford rang me up and asked me if I had had the message. When I said 'Yes,' he implored me to do as he asked, and before I could question him, he had hung up on me.

Dick examined the writing. It was in the same hand as all the letters he had seen.

"And then," Havelock went on, "I had the good sense to call up Mrs Lansdown, and learned for the first time of her daughter's disappearance."

"Did you communicate with Scotland Yard?"

"No, I didn't," confessed Havelock irritably. "I suppose I should have done, but when I found that our excellent friend, Mr Martin, had gone out in search of the young lady, I supposed that he would have taken every precaution to secure assistance. She is here, you say?"

Dick opened the door and ushered in the unexpected caller. It was daylight now, to the girl's intense relief, and with every familiar face she felt herself growing in courage. The shock of her adventure had been for a while paralysing to her mind and body, and had left her tired and incapable of grasping the full significance of her night's experience. It was light enough to search the grounds, Dick decided, and, refusing Sneed's assistance, he went alone through the farmyard towards the tombs. Ten minutes' walk brought him to the iron grille. It was locked, and obviously there was nothing to be gained by searching the vaults, for Stalletti would have made his getaway immediately after the girl's escape. The only thing to be done now was to go back by the way the girl had come and which she had described well enough to allow him to follow.

A quarter of an hour's walk brought him to the place where, as nearly as he could guess, Tom Cawler had stayed behind to meet his attacker. He quartered the ground carefully. A struggle on grass would leave few signs except to the careful observer. Presently he found what he was seeking – a torn tuft of turf, the mark of a rubber heel, a depression in the grass where somebody had lain. He went round the spot in circles, expecting to find signs of a heavy body having been dragged across the ground, but to his surprise this clue was not visible. If Cawler had been killed, and he did not doubt he had been killed, what had been done with the body? To search the innumerable clumps of wood which dotted the park was out of the question. He went back to the house to report his failure.

When he came into the room, the lawyer and Sneed were discussing something in a low tone.

"Mr Havelock is rather worried about the man whom the young lady saw," explained Sneed. "He thinks he is still in the house. That isn't my belief."

"Where is this Jesuit room?" asked Dick, and Havelock, despite his anxiety, was amused.

"The Jesuit room is a myth!" he said. "I heard that story a year ago and had an architect down to square up the house; he told me there was no space unaccounted for, and the plans prove this. Most of these Tudor houses have some sort of secret apartment, but so far as we know, there is nothing mysterious about Selford Manor except its smelly system of gas-lighting!"

"What do you intend doing?" asked Havelock after the pause which followed.

"My inclination is to return to town. Miss Lansdown must, of course, go back to her mother," said Dick.

The elder man shook his head gravely.

"I hope Miss Lansdown will agree to stay," he said. "Possibly – and naturally – she may object, but there is more in Selford's letter than I dare understand."

"You mean about not leaving the Manor for twenty-four hours?"

Havelock nodded.

"I take a very serious view of this warning," he said. "I believe there is a terrible danger lurking somewhere in the background, and I suggest – and I suppose you'll think I am a scared old man – that we stay here until tomorrow, and that Mr Sneed brings down a dozen men to patrol the grounds tonight."

Dick stared at him.

"Do you really mean this?" he asked.

"I do," said Mr Havelock, and there was no mistaking his earnestness. "Mr Sneed is of the same opinion. There have been one or two happenings in the history of this family which I think you ought to know. I won't be so melodramatic as to suggest that there is a curse overhanging the house of Selford, but it is a fact that, with the exception of the late Lord Selford, five earlier holders of the title have died violently, and in each case the death has been preceded by happenings almost as remarkable as those we have witnessed recently."

Dick smiled.

"But we're not members of the Selford family," he said.

"I think for the moment we may regard ourselves as being identical with the Selford interests," Havelock answered quickly. "There is a something very sinister in Selford's continued absence – I never realized that fact so clearly as I do now. I have been a fool to allow – and, I am afraid, to abet his wanderings. All sorts of things may have happened to him."

Not by so much as a twitch of face did Dick Martin betray his knowledge of the absent Lord Selford's secret.

"But I can't allow Miss Lansdown to stay here – " he began.

"I have thought of that, and my idea is to ask her mother to come down. The house is well stocked in the matter of furniture, and I dare say we could get temporary servants from the village. The caretaker knows everybody hereabouts."

Dick glanced at Sneed and saw, by the fat man's face, that he agreed.

"I'll go into the village and get on the phone," he said. "Anyway, I'd prefer to sleep here today than go back to town. I'm all in."

It was not so astonishing that Sybil fell in with this view, though Selford's letter had no influence on her decision. The reaction after such a night was painfully evident. She was tired to the point of exhaustion and could hardly keep awake.

Sneed drew his friend aside.

"This will suit us all right. I shall get a few hours' sleep, and we are pretty near to Cody's place. I'm afraid we shall have an all day session there."

Dick started violently. He had almost forgotten the horror in his anxiety for the girl. Eventually it was agreed that Havelock should go up to town in his car and bring Mrs Lansdown down with him.

The news of her daughter's safety had already been conveyed to her, and after the lawyer had left Dick went again to the village and telephoned to her. She was eager to come at once, but he asked her to wait for Havelock's arrival.

27

There was much for Sneed to do before he could find the rest he so greatly needed. After a hasty breakfast he met the police chief of Sussex, and together they motored over to Gallows Hill, carrying a warrant for the arrest of the scientist. But the bird had flown, and the house was in charge of an odd man who had been employed to do jobs about the grounds. He had, he said, no knowledge whatever of the doctor or of any other inmate of the house. The man lived in a little cottage about a quarter of a mile away from the doctor's house, and his story was that he had been awakened early in the morning by Stalletti, who had given him a key and told him to go to Gallows Cottage and stay there until he returned.

A search of the house revealed no fresh information. The doctor's bed had not been slept in, and the two beds in the little room were also untenanted.

"It would be a very difficult charge to prove, anyway," said the Sussex officer as they left the house. "Unless you found the pellets in his possession, you could hardly charge him with administering dangerous drugs. And even then you'd have to prove they were dangerous. They may have been a sedative. You say that the young lady met this man in peculiar circumstances, and while she was in a very nervous state?"

"She met him, to be exact," said Sneed sarcastically, "in a tomb in the bowels of the earth at two o'clock in the morning, which, I submit, are circumstances which incline a young lady to feel a trifle on the nervous side."

"In the Selford tomb? You didn't tell me that," said the Sussex man resentfully. For there is, between Scotland Yard and the provincial police, a certain amount of friction, which it would be ungenerous to ascribe to jealousy and untruthful to explain as well founded.

Until midday Sneed was at the Weald House, in consultation with the officer who had been called in from Scotland Yard to take charge of the case.

"No, there are no marks on the woman. She died from fright – at least, that is the doctor's opinion," said the Yard man. "The other fellow was beaten to death. I've searched the orchard, it is simply littered with spent shells from an automatic pistol. How do you account for that?"

Sneed told him of the fusillade which had met them when they attempted to pursue the unknown trespasser.

"We found eighteen empty cartridge cases; there are probably another one or two knocking about which we haven't picked up yet," said the Scotland Yard man. "Can you account for the ladder which we found against the house?"

Sneed explained that phenomenon in a few words.

"Humph!" said the Yard man. "It is queer about Cody. He's on the register."

"Don't use those American expressions," said Sneed testily, and the Yard man grinned, for he had spent two years in New York and had added to the vocabulary of police headquarters."

"Anyway, he's in the Records Office. He was convicted twenty-five years ago of obtaining money by false pretences in the name of Bertram; he was one of the first individuals in England to run a correspondence school, and he caught some unfortunate person for a thousand pounds on the pretence that he could teach him the art of hypnotism. He and a fellow Stalletti were in it, but Stalletti got away – "

"Stalletti?" Sneed looked at him open-mouthed. "That Italian doctor?"

"He's the fellow," nodded Inspector Wilson. "If you remember, our people caught Stalletti for vivisecting without a licence, but that was a few years later. He is a clever devil, Stalletti."

"'Clever' is not the word," said Sneed grimly. "But it is news to me that they were acquainted."

"Acquainted! Stalletti came here twice a week. I've been talking to some of the servants, who were given a holiday last night and told not to come back until ten o'clock this morning. There was something dirty going on here and Cody wanted them out of the way."

Sneed took his hand and shook it solemnly.

"You've got the making of a detective in you," he said. "I discovered that before I went into the house last night!"

As he was going: "By the way, Martin has been here. He came to retrieve his car. He's driven it flat into Horsham to get new tyres and he wanted me to ask you to wait for him."

Sneed strolled down to the lodge gates and had not long to wait when Dick's machine came flying along the road.

"Jump in; I'm going to Selford," said Martin. "Mrs Lansdown arrived half an hour ago. Did you find Stalletti?"

"No. That bird is doing a little quick flying – and he's wise!"

"I didn't expect he would wait for you."

"Do you know he was a friend of Cody's?" asked Sneed.

He was a little annoyed when his information failed to produce the sensation he had anticipated. Dick Martin knew this and more.

"Oh yes. Old and tried friends – but not by the same jury. I'd give a lot of money to have Stalletti's key!"

"His what?"

"His key," repeated Dick, dodging round a farmer's cart and narrowly escaping destruction from a speedster coming from the other direction. "He has the fifth key; Lord Selford has probably the sixth; and X, the great unknown, has the seventh. I'm not quite sure about Lord Selford," he went on, and the other listened thunderstricken. "But if I'd got to Cape Town four or five days before I did, I should have known for sure."

"Is Selford in this?" demanded Sneed.

"Very much in it," was the reply, "but not quite so much as Stalletti. Forgive me being mysterious, Sneed, but nature intended me to be a writer of mystery stories, and I like sometimes to escape from the humdrum of detective investigation into the realms of romance."

"Where is Cawler?"

"The Lord knows!" said Dick cheerfully. "My first idea was that he was responsible for the murders, but maybe I'm wrong. He hated his aunt – that, by the way, was Mrs Cody – but I don't think he hated her well enough to commit wilful murder. He was certainly very good to Sybil Lansdown."

Sneed grinned.

"Which goes a long way with you, Dick."

"Farther than you could see," admitted Dick shamelessly.

Mrs Lansdown was not visible when they arrived. She had gone up to the room where her daughter was sleeping and had not come down, Mr Havelock told them.

"Have you arranged to get the police down?" he asked.

"There will be a dozen hard-eating men quartered in this kitchen tonight," said Sneed good-humouredly.

Mr Havelock put down the book he had been reading, and rising, stretched himself painfully.

"I'm worried sick. I'll confess that to you, Captain Sneed," he said. "Our friend Martin thinks I am romancing, but I can tell you that I shall be a very relieved man this time tomorrow morning."

He strode up and down the room, his hands behind him, his high forehead wrinkled in a frown.

"Lord Selford is not in London," he said without preliminary. "At any rate, he is not at the Ritz-Carlton. They have not seen him and know nothing about him."

"Has he ever stayed at the Ritz-Carlton?" asked Dick quickly.

"No – that is the extraordinary thing about it. I asked that very question. It was on an impulse that I stopped as I was passing this morning. You will remember that I have had several letters from him on Ritz-Carlton paper?"

Dick nodded.

"But he has never stayed there; I could have told you that," he said. "Have you ever sent money to him there?"

"Yes," said the lawyer immediately. "About two years ago he rang me up on the telephone. I recognized his voice the moment he spoke. He said he was going to Scotland to fish and asked me if I would send him some American money – a very considerable sum – to the hotel."

"How much?"

"Twenty thousand dollars," said Havelock. "I didn't like it."

"Did you ask him to see you?"

"I didn't ask him, I begged him. In fact," he confessed, "I threatened to resign my trusteeship unless he came in to see me or allowed me to see him; just about then I was getting a little nervous."

"What did he say?"

Mr Havelock shrugged his broad shoulders.

"He laughed. He has a peculiar, weak, giggling sort of laugh that I remember ever since he was a boy. It is inimitable, and is the one sure proof to me that the doubts I had privately entertained had no foundation."

"Did you send the money?"

"I had to," said Mr Havelock in a tone of despair. "After all, I was merely a servant of the estate, and he moves so rapidly as to allow of no delay in dispatching. It was then I began to think of sending somebody to 'pick him up' – that is the police term, isn't it?"

Dick thought for a while.

"Tell me one thing: when he called you up last night, did he tell you where he was speaking from?"

"I knew," was the reply. "It was from a call office. The operator invariably tells you when a call office is coming through. The strange thing is that only a few days ago he was reported at Damascus. We have been working out the times, and we have concluded that by flying to Constantinople and catching the Oriental express, he could have reached London half an hour before he telephoned to me."

The conversation was interrupted by the arrival of Mrs Lansdown, who had come from her daughter. Sybil's mother looked worn, but there was happiness in the tired eyes, which told of the relief she had experienced after the most terrible night of strain and anxiety.

"I don't understand what it is all about," she said, "but thank God my little girl is safe. Have you found the chauffeur?"

"Cawler? No, he has not been seen since Sybil left him."

"You don't think anything has happened?" she asked nervously.

"I don't know. I shouldn't think so," replied Dick with a reassuring smile. "Cawler is quite able to look after himself, and I don't doubt that if there was a fight he came off best."

Later in the afternoon there arrived further news of Stalletti. He had been seen by a village constable soon after he had aroused his hired man. Apparently Stalletti had a small car which he was in the habit of driving about the neighbourhood, and the cycling constable had seen him speeding in the direction of London.

"Speeding" is hardly the term that could be properly applied, for the machine did thirty miles an hour with difficulty and had the habit of going dead for no ascertainable cause. Stalletti was looking wild and agitated and was talking to himself; he was cranking the car when the constable came up with him, and the policeman thought he had been drinking, for he seemed to be abnormally excited and scarcely noticed the advent of the cyclist.

"That bears out to a large extent my theory," said Dick. "Stalletti is a devil, but a shrewd devil. He knows that the sands are running out, and with him, as with Cody, it is a case of *sauve qui peut.*"

He managed to get a few hours' sleep, and in the evening he made a very careful survey of the house, particularly of the sleeping quarters which had been assigned to the party. The upper floor was reached by a broad carved staircase, Elizabethan in design and execution, which terminated at a broad oblong landing, from which ran the two corridors into which the bedrooms opened. There were eight massive doors, four on each side. The corridor was lighted by long windows which looked down into a courtyard, formed by two wings of the building. In one of these was a self-contained suite, which had been the late Lord Selford's private apartments, and in which, in point of fact, he had died. The other wing had been converted into servants' quarters. There were no apartments above, the bedrooms being extremely lofty and running up to within a few feet of the roof. Facing the stairs was the "State Apartment", as it was called, which had once been the principal bedroom of the house, and this had been assigned to Sybil and her mother.

28

Whilst the ladies were walking in the park after tea, Dick went from room to room and made a very thorough examination of windows and walls. He had procured a builder's tape measure, and, with the assistance of one of the police officers who had arrived from London, he measured the room both inside and out, and compared his figures with those he obtained from the two apartments which flanked the state chamber. The difference was so slight as to preclude any possibility of there being a secret passage between the walls. These, as is usual in the Elizabethan buildings, were very thick and seemed solid enough.

The state apartment was a large room, rather overpoweringly furnished, with an old-fashioned four-poster bed set upon a dais. The walls were hung with tapestries; a few old pieces of furniture comprised its contents, and had the floor been covered with rushes it might have stood for an Elizabethan bedroom without one modern touch.

He pulled aside the long velvet curtains that hid the windows and saw that they were very heavily barred, and called up the caretaker.

"Yes, sir, these are the only windows in the house that have bars," said the man. "The late Lord Selford had them put after a burglary. You see, the porch is just below, and it is easy to get into the state room."

Dick pulled open the leaded windows and examined the bars closely. They were firmly fixed and set so close that it was impossible for any but a child to squeeze through. As he was shutting the windows, Sneed came into the room.

"The ladies are sleeping here, aren't they?" asked the stout man, and nodded his approval of the bars. "They'll be safe enough. I'll have a man in the corridor all night, one in the hall, and two in the grounds. Personally, I'm not worried about trouble coming tonight, unless his lordship brings it with him. What time is he expected?"

"Between six and seven in the morning," said Dick, and Captain Sneed grunted his satisfaction.

There was one other part of the house that Dick Martin was anxious to see, and here the caretaker was his guide. There was, he learned, a range of cellars running half the width of the main block. These were reached through an underground kitchen, one section was set aside as a wine cellar and was, he found, well stocked. There were no lights here save those which he carried, and, unlike many other cellars of these Elizabethan houses, the roof was not vaulted. Great oaken beams ran across the cellar, and these supported heavy wooden slats, black with age.

Apart from the wine cellar, this underground portion of Selford Manor was empty except for three large beer barrels, which had arrived only a few days before. He tapped them one by one, and on an excuse sent the caretaker upstairs. Dick's sense of smell was abnormal, and when he sniffed it was not the smell of beer that reached his nostrils.

Looking round, he saw in a dark corner a small case opener. It was very new. Climbing the steps, he closed and bolted the door, and, returning to the barrels, prised open the end of one. The fumes now became overpowering. Dipping in his hand he ran his fingers through the glistening white flakes and grinned. Then, replacing the lid, he went up the steps.

This inspection satisfied Dick on many points. He went up to the hall and, passing to the back of the building, took his car and drove down to the lodge gates, returning on foot, not by the drive, but through the plantation which bordered the eastern portion of the estate.

The hour of crisis was at hand. He felt that the atmosphere was electric, and this night would settle, one way or the other, the mystery of Lord Selford's long disappearance.

Before dinner he had an opportunity of a talk with the girl. They strode up and down the broad lawn before the house.

"Oh yes, I slept," she said with a smile. And then, unexpectedly: "Mr Martin, I have given you an awful lot of trouble."

"Me?" He was genuinely surprised. "I can't see that you have given me more trouble than other people," he went on lamely. "You have certainly caused me a lot of anxiety, but that is only natural."

There was a pause.

"Do you feel that way about all – your cases?" she asked, not looking at him.

"This isn't a case – Sybil," he said, a little huskily. "I have a personal interest here. Your safety means more to me than anything else in the world."

She shot one quick glance at him.

"And am I safe now?" she asked, and when he did not reply: "Why are we staying here tonight?"

"Mr Havelock thinks – " he began.

"Mr Havelock is frightened," she said quietly. "He believes that whoever these terrible people are, he has been chosen as the next victim."

"Of whom is he afraid?" asked Dick.

"Of Stalletti," she shuddered.

He looked at her in amazement.

"Why do you say that? Mr Havelock has told you?"

She nodded.

"Men will say things to women that they will never confess to men," she said. "Do you know that Mr Havelock believes that Lord Selford is entirely under Stalletti's influence? And, what is more, he thinks that – but he will tell you himself. Do you know why we are staying at Selford Manor?"

"I only know about a message that came to Havelock," said Dick.

"We're staying here because it is a fortress – the only fortress which can keep this horrible man at bay. Why I am included in the invitation, I don't know. But Mr Havelock is very insistent upon the point. Lord Selford cannot possibly be interested in me."

"He is your cousin," he said significantly, and she stared at him.

"What does that mean?"

"It means," Dick spoke slowly, "and this thought has only occurred to me recently, that, if Lord Selford dies, you are the heiress-at-law."

She was speechless with astonishment.

"But that isn't so, surely? Mr Havelock hinted to me that Selford had probably married. And I'm a very distant relation."

He nodded.

"The only relation," he said; "and now you will understand just why you have been threatened. You told me Mr Cody had offered you a paper to sign. There is no doubt at all that that paper was either some deed of gift or a will. Cody was in the Selford business up to his neck."

"But where is Lord Selford?"

"I don't know," he replied simply. "I can only guess – and fear."

Her eyes opened wide.

"You don't mean – he's dead?" she gasped.

"He may be. I'm not sure. Perhaps it would be better if he were."

Mr Havelock was approaching him, trouble on his rugged face, a frown of perplexity making a furrow in his forehead.

"What time do you expect Selford to arrive?" asked Dick.

The lawyer shook his head.

"If he arrives at all I shall be a happy man," he said. "For the moment I have not any great hope, only a vague kind of apprehension. What news will the morning bring to us? I'd give my small fortune to be a day older than I am. There is no news, I suppose, about Stalletti?"

"None," said Dick. " The police are looking for him, and he will find it difficult to escape."

The caretaker came out at that moment to announce that a meal had been got ready, and they went into the library, where it had been served.

The dinner, for which the caretaker and his wife were equally apologetic, was of the simplest order. They dined on cold viands, of a quality in odd contrast to the wine which came up from the cellar. After the meal was over, Dick took the girl into the rose garden at the back of the house, and for a long time Mrs Lansdown watched them pacing up and down the gravelled walk, deep in earnest conversation.

Presently the girl came in alone and spoke to her mother, and the two of them returned to where Dick Martin was pacing the path, his hands behind him, his chin on his breast.

When he at last appeared on the lawn before the house, he found Mr Havelock and Sneed were discussing the disposition of the Scotland Yard men. It was growing dark, the light showed in the window of a distant cottage. Dick looked up at the sky. Darkness would fall in an hour; after that –

"Who is going for a walk to the tombs?" he asked.

Mr Havelock did not receive the suggestion with enthusiasm.

"It is too dark," he said nervously. "And we can't leave these people alone in the house."

"Our men will look after them," said Dick. "Anyway, they have gone to bed. Mrs Lansdown sent her excuses."

"I think they're quite safe," said Mr Havelock, looking up at the barred windows. "I confess that as time goes on I am considerably doubtful as to the wisdom of spending the night in this wretched place. I suppose – " He hesitated and laughed. "I was going to do a very cowardly thing and suggest that I should go home. As I am the only person who need stay, that idea would hardly appeal to you gentlemen. The truth is," he said frankly, "I'm nervous – horribly nervous! I feel as if there is some fearful shadow lurking in every bush, a ghastly shape behind every clump of trees."

"We'll not go to the tombs," said Dick, "but we will go as far as the valley. There are one or two things I would like to ask you; the topography here is not very familiar to me and you may help me."

The three men went through the farmyard, and Dick stopped only to pat the chained watch-dog who had served Sybil Lansdown so well. So they passed into what he had come to call "the valley".

The sky was clear; the sun had gone down, but it was light enough to see even distant objects. And here, as they strolled, Mr Havelock learned for the first time of the secret behind Lew Pheeney's death.

"But this is amazing!" he said in astonishment. "There was nothing in the newspapers about his having been asked to pick a lock – of course, it was the lock of the Selford tomb!"

"The information that doesn't come out at inquests would fill Miss Lansdown's library," said Sneed. "Maybe it will all come some day."

They walked on in silence for a long time. Evidently Mr Havelock was cogitating this news.

"I wish I had known before," he said eventually. "I might have been able to give you a great deal of assistance. I suppose he didn't tell you who was his employer?"

Dick shook his head.

"No, but we can guess."

"Stalletti?" asked Havelock quickly.

"I should imagine so. I can't think of anybody else."

They stopped at the place where the struggle had occurred between Tom Cawler and the Awful Thing, and Dick turned slowly round and round until his eyes had roved the full circle of the view.

"What is that place?" He pointed to a white scar showing above a grassy ridge.

"Those are the Selford Quarries," said the lawyer; "they are not worked today and represent a liability. We have had to close the road above them."

Dick thought for a moment.

"You don't feel like coming on to the tombs?" he asked, concealing a smile.

"I certainly do not," cried Mr Havelock with energy. "There's nothing in the world I wish to do less than to go poking round that ghastly place at this hour of the night! Shall we return?"

They walked back to the house; here the two Scotland Yard men who were on guard outside the house reported that Mrs Lansdown had opened the window of her room and had asked if she could be called at six in the morning.

"Let us go inside," said Havelock; "we shall disturb them with our voices."

They went back to the dining-hall and Havelock ordered up a quart of rare champagne. The hand that raised the glass to his lips trembled a little. The strain, he admitted, was beginning to tell upon him.

"Whatever happens, I am through with the Selford estate from tonight," he said; "and if this wretched young man does turn up – and I very much doubt whether he will keep this appointment – I shall hand him over my trust with the greatest relief."

"In which room are you sleeping?" asked Dick.

"I have chosen one of the wing rooms that faces up the corridor. It is part of the suite which the late Lord Selford occupied, and is by far the most comfortable. Though I'm not so sure it is the safest, because I'm rather isolated. I wanted to suggest that you have a man in the corridor."

"I've already arranged that," said Sneed, putting down his glass and smacking his lips with relish. "That's good wine. I don't think I have tasted anything better."

"Could you drink another bottle?" said Mr Havelock hopefully, and Sneed chuckled.

"You want an excuse to open another bottle, Mr Havelock!" he accused. "And I'll give it to you!"

Under the influence of the second bottle of wine the lawyer became more his normal self.

"The matter is still a tangle to me," he said. "What Cody had to do with Selford, or in what manner this wretched Italian – "

"Greek," said Sneed quietly. "He calls himself Italian, but he's of Greek origin; I've established that fact. As to their connection, I'll tell you something." He folded his arms on the table and leaned across. "You remember sending Lord Selford to school?" he said slowly.

"To a private school – yes." Mr Havelock was patently astonished at the question.

"Do you remember the name of the schoolmaster?"

Havelock frowned.

"I think I do," he said slowly. "Mr Bertram."

"He used to be Bertram, but later he took the name of Cody," said Sneed, and the other man's jaw dropped.

"Cody?" he said incredulously. "Do you mean to say that Cody and Bertram, Selford's tutor, are one and the same person?"

It was Dick who answered.

"And now let me ask you a question, Mr Havelock. When this boy was quite young, had he a nurse?"

"Why, of course," replied Havelock.

"Do you remember her name?"

Again the lawyer searched his memory.

"I can't be sure, but I have an idea it was Crowther or some such name."

"Cawler?" suggested Dick.

"Yes, I think it was." The lawyer thought a while. "I'm certain it was. The name is familiar to me. I've heard of some other person called Cawler. Of course, Cody's chauffeur!"

"She was Cawler's aunt," said Dick. "Originally she was a nurse in the employ of the late Lord Selford, and she had charge of the boy. Does it strike you as significant that Cody should marry this uneducated and uncouth woman?"

There was a deep silence.

"How did you find this out?"

"By an examination of Cody's papers. Whoever murdered that wretched man carried away all the documents that were in his desk. But they omitted to search a box in which Mrs Cody kept her private treasures. Probably they thought that she was not the type of woman who would keep any private correspondence; but the letters we found leave no doubt at all that she was Lord Selford's nurse, and that Cody was his tutor. You've never seen Cody?"

Havelock shook his head.

"Are you also aware," said Dick slowly, "that Stalletti was, on two occasions, called in to Selford Manor in his capacity as a medical man to treat Lord Selford for alcoholism?"

"You amaze me!" gasped the lawyer. "Selford's doctor was Sir John Finton. I never knew that he had a local man. When did you learn all this?"

Dick looked at Sneed, who took out his pocket-case, selected a paper, and passed it across to the lawyer. It was the paper Dick had found in the box.

"But in what way do these affect the present Lord Selford and his wanderings?" asked Havelock in a tone of wonder. "The thing is inexplicable! The more information I get on this subject, the more obscure the whole affair seems to be!"

"Lord Selford will tell us that in the morning," said Dick briskly and looked at his watch. "And now I think we'll go to bed. I am a very tired man."

Sneed dragged himself from the table and flopped into a deep chair before the fire, which had been lighted in their absence.

"This is my pitch, and it is going to take a good man to get me out of it!"

29

It was half-past ten when Dick and the lawyer went upstairs to their rooms, and after he had seen Mr Havelock safely in his suite and had heard the key turned, he went into his own apartment, shut and locked the door, and lit a candle.

He waited ten minutes and then, noiselessly unlocking the door, he stepped out into the corridor. The detective on duty saluted him silently as he took out a key and relocked the door from the outside. Then he passed down the stairs and into the hall, where Sneed was waiting for him. Without a word, Dick unfastened the door of the room in which Sybil had seen the strange apparition, and they went in together.

The blinds here had been drawn by the caretaker; one of these, at the farther end of the room, Dick raised and pulled back the curtain.

"Wait in the hall, Sneed, and don't so much as cough until I shout. We may have to wait till daylight, but it's an even break that the man with the beard will come back."

Noiselessly he passed through the dark night and, climbing up to one of the raised flowerbeds, he took up a position where he could see the interior of the room. His theory might very well be absurd; on the other hand, it might prove to be the keystone of the solution he had constructed.

Time passed slowly, but he did not move, his face against the window-pane, his eyes staring into the darkness of the room. Far away in the still night he heard a church clock strike midnight, and, after an eternity, the half-hour. He began to think that his night was to be wasted, when suddenly, near the fireplace, there appeared on the floor a long, thin line of light. Holding his breath, he waited. The line broadened. And then, by the faint illumination provided, he saw the big hearthstone turn on a pivot, and a head appeared above the floor level.

It was a dreadful face he saw. The staring eyes, the straggling, ragged beard, the huge, naked arm that rested for a second on the edge of the floor, were monstrously unreal. The Thing placed the candle he had been holding on the floor, and without an effort drew himself up until he was clear of the pit from which he had climbed.

Except for a pair of ragged short breeches he was naked. Dick gazed, spellbound, as the giant crouched and reached down a hand. And then another huge form came up, and the second of the monstrous beings appeared.

He was taller than the first. His round face was expressionless, and, unlike his companion, his skin was smooth, his head almost shaven.

Dick stared and felt his heart beating faster. For the first time in his life he was really afraid. Shading the candle with his huge hand, the first of the men moved stealthily along the panelled wall, the second, a taller figure, crouching behind him. The man with the candle was feeling the panelling.

And then something happened.

Dick found it hard to suppress a cry of astonishment as he saw one of the panels swing open, revealing the face of a small cupboard. The bearded thing took something out and showed it to the other, and their heads were almost together as they seemed to gloat over their discovery.

And then, even from where he was standing, he heard somebody rattle on the door of the room, and cursed the bungling man who had interrupted this amazing conference.

For, as the door shook, the light went out. Dick flew along the stone path into the hall, and saw Sneed, his hand on the door.

"Somebody's in there," said the fat man.

"If you'd only waited a second!" hissed Dick furiously, as he unlocked the door and flung it open.

The room was empty when they turned on the lights.

"Look!" said Sneed, pointing to the panelled door.

"I've already seen that."

Briefly and a little cantankerously, he described what he had seen.

He expected to find that the panel concealed a safe of some kind, and he was amazed when he discovered that it was no more than a big wooden cupboard filled with what seemed to be an accumulation of rubbish. He pulled out the contents and put them on the floor. There was an old wooden horse with a broken leg; a gaily-painted India rubber ball; a few children's skittles; and part of a clockwork train, the engine of which was missing.

With the assistance of Sneed, he tried to turn the hearthstone, but it was immovable.

"Stay here," said Dick, and ran out of the room through the hall into the grounds.

The dog yapped its fierce warnings as he crossed the farmyard, but a muttered word quietened him. He took a short-cut, vaulting the low wall, and reached the valley, stopping now and again to look round in search of something.

Then he began a wide circuit of the valley, keeping as far as possible from observation, and it was nearly an hour before he began the steep ascent to the wood in which the tombs were concealed. Dick moved cautiously, choosing every footfall, listening at every step; but it was not until he was nearly clear of the wood that he heard the sound of crooning voices.

There was a familiar lilt to the tune; a memory that took him back nearly thirty years – it was the sound of children singing.

Nearer and nearer he crept, slipping from tree to tree, his senses taut. The sweat was running down his face; he had to take out his handkerchief and wipe his eyes before he could see. He passed from one tree to another until at last he reached the cover of a giant elm, and from there he looked out upon the moonlit clearing.

The gate of the tomb was wide open, but this he did not see for some time. All his attention was concentrated upon the three men who, hand in hand, were moving round in a circle, two treble voices and a deep, unmusical bass, singing as they solemnly walked:

"Poor Jinny is a-weeping,

Poor Jinny is a-weeping…"

His heart almost stopped beating at the sight. It was like a bad dream; and yet there was something so pathetic in the sight that he felt the tears rising to his eyes.

The two half-naked figures he recognized instantly. The third little man he could not immediately place, till he turned his unshaven face towards the moon. It was Tom Cawler!

Then of a sudden the song ceased, and they squatted down on the ground and passed something from hand to hand. Presently Dick saw what it was – a clockwork locomotive! The two half-nude men chuckled over it delightedly, uttering childish, unintelligible sounds, whilst Tom Cawler stared straight ahead, his face set, his eyes open wide, till it seemed to the watcher that he was the most terrible of the three.

The interruption which came was startling in its unexpectedness. A soft whistle came from the wood so close at hand that Dick jumped round. Its effect upon the group was extraordinary. The two giants came up to their feet, cringing away from the sound, and when Dick looked again, Tom Cawler had disappeared.

Again the whistle, and the two great shapes crouched down, and even from that distance Dick saw that they were trembling violently. The sound of a breaking twig, and a man stepped into the clearing.

It was Stalletti.

In one hand he held a whirling dog-whip, in the other the moon gleamed on something bright and sinister.

"Ah! so, my little children, I have found you, in what strange circumstances! Extraordinary and bizarre, is it not? Come, Beppo."

The lash curled above their heads as the bigger man crouched lower to the earth.

"Come, you!"

He said something in Greek, which Dick could not understand, and immediately the two huge shapes shuffled after him and passed into the wood. Still Dick did not move. Where was Cawler? He had vanished as into the ground. And then suddenly the detective saw him, moving swiftly in the shadow of the trees, following the course which Stalletti and his slaves had taken. In another instant Dick was on their heels.

For a moment he had been paralysed by the fantastic sight, but now the spell was broken. Whatever happened, Stalletti should not escape. He did not see Cawler, but knew that he was somewhere ahead in the darkness, moving, as Dick had moved, from tree to tree, silently, ominously, for the unconscious man who by some mischance had failed to see him.

They did not follow the steep path down to the valley, but went along the slope. The detective, who had not explored the wood, wondered where the chase would end. Once, as the trees thinned, he saw the two cowering figures following Stalletti, but they were lost to view again, and he did not sight them until he heard the harsh purr of a motor engine, and dashed forward. He was too late. There was some sort of road here, of which he knew nothing, and the car was moving along this. As he looked he saw a figure shoot out of the bushes and grip the back of the machine.

Now he located the road; it was that which ran over the top of Selford Quarry. He saw the white gash of the chalk cliff in the moonlight as he flew along in pursuit of the car. The road was bad, he guessed, and they could not make any great speed, and Dick Martin was something of a runner.

The rough roadway began to climb, and this gave him an additional advantage, for, heavily laden – more heavily than Stalletti at the wheel imagined – the machine slowed perceptibly, and he was gaining hand over hand, when he saw the man that was hanging on to the back suddenly pull himself over the hood.

What followed he could only guess. There was a scream from Stalletti, and suddenly the car lurched violently to the left and broke through a clump of bushes. For a second there was silence, and then a horrible crash. Dick ran to the edge of the quarry and saw the car tumbling over and over down the almost precipitous slope. Down, down, down it went, into the deep, still pool in which the moon was reflected.

30

Dick looked round for a safe way to the bottom, and presently was clambering down a projecting shoulder of the hill. He reached the edge of the lake as a figure came wading ashore, blubbering and sobbing in grief and fury. Dick seized him by the shoulder and swung him round.

"Cawler!" he said.

"My God! My God! He's dead!" sobbed the chauffeur. "Both of 'em! And that swine! I ought to have killed him first!"

"Where are they?"

The man pointed with a shaking hand to a small triangular object in the centre of the lake.

"The car turned over. I tried to pull him out," he wailed. "If I'd only killed him that night I found what they'd done! Do something, Mr Martin." He gripped Dick frenziedly. "Save him. I don't care what happens to me. Perhaps we could get the car turned over?"

Without a word, Dick threw off his coat and waded into the shallow water, followed by the half-demented Cawler. At the first attempt he realized that the task was impossible; in turning, the machine had wedged itself under a projecting rock. He dived down and sought to pull clear the huge creature his hand touched; and all the time Tom Cawler was sobbing his fury and anguish.

"If I'd only killed him when I found out! That night I listened at the window when Cody was there. I killed him tonight. You can take me for it, if you like, Martin. I smashed in his head with a spanner."

"Who killed Cody?"

"My brother killed him. God! I'm glad of it! He killed him because Stalletti told him to."

"Your brother?" said Dick, hardly believing the evidence of his ears.

"My brother – the big fellow," sobbed the man. "Stalletti experimented on him first, before he took the other boy."

It needed all Dick's strength to drag to safety this man, half mad with sorrow and remorse. Leaving him at the edge of the lake, Martin began to work his way back to the valley. No assistance he could procure could rescue the three men who were pinned down beneath the car, but he must make some attempt.

As he mounted the slope towards the farm he heard a police whistle blow shrilly, and almost immediately there came a strange red glow from behind the trees. Dick threw away the coat he was carrying and sprinted, but before he could reach the farmyard wall he saw the red flames leaping up to the sky.

Again the police whistle shrilled. And now, as he turned the corner of the farm buildings, Dick Martin saw…

Selford Manor was ablaze from one end to the other. Red and white tongues of flame were leaping from each window. The lawn was as bright as though day had dawned.

Mr Havelock, an overcoat over his pyjamas, was running up and down frenziedly.

"Save the women!" he raved. "Can't you force those bars and get them out?"

Captain Sneed stood apathetically by. He was more than apathetic, he was callous. He was smoking his big pipe with a solemn indifference.

"The women, I tell you!" screamed Havelock, waving his hands to the barred windows of the state room, from which the flames were now roaring.

Dick's hand fell on his arm.

"You needn't worry, Mr Havelock," he said quietly. "Neither Mrs Lansdown nor her daughter is in the house."

The lawyer stared round at him.

"Not in the house?" he gasped.

"I sent them to London much earlier in the evening – in fact, when we were searching the valley a few hours ago," said Dick, and nodded to his companion.

Mr Sneed took his pipe from his mouth, knocked out the ashes, and became instantly a competent police official.

"Your name is Arthur Elwood Havelock, and I am Chief Inspector John Sneed of Scotland Yard. I shall take you into custody on a charge of murder and incitement to murder, and I caution you that what you now say may be taken down and used in evidence against you at your trial."

Havelock opened his mouth to speak, but only a hoarse groan escaped him. And then, as another detective caught him by the arm, he collapsed in an unconscious heap on the ground.

They carried him down to the porter's lodge, and began their search. About his neck was a thin steel chain, and to this were attached what Dick expected to see – two keys of peculiar design. Under the stimulus of a glass of brandy, Mr Havelock had recovered, and he was a very indignant man.

"This is the most monstrous charge that has ever been concocted," he said violently. "For the life of me, I can't understand what you mean by such a disgraceful – "

"Spare us your eloquence, Mr Havelock," said Dick coldly. "It will save you a lot of trouble when I tell you that I have known, from the day I saw a certain photograph in Cape Town, that my chase of Lord Selford was a fake organized by you to allay suspicion. Probably somebody else had been inquiring as to the whereabouts of Selford, and you thought it would be an excellent proof of your *bona fides* if you sent a fully fledged detective to hunt him down. And, having arrived at this decision, you, with the connivance of Cody, sent his chauffeur, Tom Cawler, to act as hare to my hounds. I happen to know that Cawler was your messenger, because he incautiously showed himself on the balcony of a Cape Town hotel and was snapped by a press photographer. I recognized him at once, and from that moment

I have been privately engaged in discovering the mystery of Lord Selford's fate."

The lawyer swallowed hard, and then, in a quivering voice:"I'll admit that I have acted very foolishly in regard to Selford. He was of a weak intellect, and I placed him in the care of a doctor – "

"You gave him to Stalletti for his damnable experiments!" said Dick sternly. "And in order to test whether Stalletti's method would be successful, you handed over another child – the nephew of Mrs Cody, and brother of Tom Cawler. I have just come from the man. He recognized his brother that night he defended Sybil Lansdown, and, calling him by an old pet name they had used as children, awakened in the poor soul a memory of the past. For that crime alone, Havelock, you shall go to the scaffold! Not for the murder of Cody, which you superintended; not for firing Selford Manor – you sent those three barrels of naphthaline which I found – but for the killing of two human souls!"

The white-faced man licked his lips.

"You will have to prove – " he began.

And then, unconsciously, his hand strayed to his neck. When he found the chain had gone, beads of perspiration rolled down his pallid face. He made two attempts to say something, and again dropped into the arms of the attendant detectives.

31

"Seven keys," said Dick, as, in the early light of morning, they walked towards the tombs. "Cody had one; Silva, the gardener, had one; Mrs Cody had another; Havelock, being the chief conspirator, had two. By the way, have they got Stalletti out of the lake? He has the sixth, and if I am not mistaken you will find the seventh hanging round the neck of Cawler's brother."

They had to wait an hour in the wood until the rescue party had done their work. The sun was rising as they put two dripping wet keys into Dick's hand.

"And these make seven," he said.

Down to the tomb they went. The door of one of the little chapels was wide open, and Dick stopped to flash his lamp inside. He threw the light on a square hole in one corner of the grim apartment.

"There is a subterranean passage that leads under the hill and terminates beneath the fireplace of what used to be, in poor little Selford's days, the playroom of the Manor. It is probably the only part of the house that the poor fellow remembered. The three men have been hiding here since the night Stalletti made his last attempt on the tomb. He had Selford with him, but, in the haste of his escape, he left his victim behind."

"Why did Selford visit the room?" asked Sneed in surprise.

"The poor creature wanted his toys – that is all. These two half-mad creatures were mentally children. They had only children's amusements and children's fears – that was the hold Stalletti had on them."

The two men stood in silence before the grim door of the big tomb, while Dick fitted and turned key after key. The seventh lock snicked back, and as he pulled the heavy door swung slowly open.

He was the first into the chamber, and made for the stone casket. Lifting the heavy lid carefully, he set it down. Within the casket was a small steel box, and this he took out.

A careful survey of the cell revealed nothing further, and they brought the box into the bright sunlight, locked the tomb, and walked back past the still smoking ruins of Selford Manor to the lodge. Havelock had been removed to Horsham, and already the local police were on the spot and were making inquiries into the tragedy of the lake.

The steel box took some time to open, but presently the lid was forced back and Dick removed a roll which proved to be a school exercise book, every page of which was filled with close writing.

"This is in Cody's hand. He was evidently the scribe," said Sneed, when he examined the book. "Read it, Martin."

Dick settled down in a chair and began the curious story of the Door with Seven Locks.

32

"This statement is written by Henry Colston Bertram, commonly called Bertram Cody, with the knowledge, approval, and agreement of those persons whose signatures appear hereunder. It was agreed on the night of March 4th in the year 1901 that such a statement should be put into writing, so that, in the event of discovery, no one of these signatories aforesaid should be regarded as being less implicated than the others, and further, to prevent any one of the said signatories from turning State evidence at the expense of the others.

"Gregory, Viscount Selford, died on the 14th November before the date this narrative was agreed upon. He was a man of extraordinary character, and it was his intention, as he confided to his lawyer, Mr Arthur Havelock, that his property should be converted into gold and should be laid in the tomb which was occupied by the founder of the Selford family, and in which Lord Selford designed that he should also be buried. And in order that his money should not come into the possession of his son until he was 25, he intended that this money should be placed in the vault with him, which was to be fastened by a door with seven locks, one key being given to each of seven executors. The old door with seven locks was accordingly taken down and a new door, a faithful copy of the first, was ordered from the firm of Rizini, of Milan. Lord Selford's scheme was obviously impossible of execution in view of the laws of succession, but although this fact was pointed out to him, he persisted in his design. He confided his plans, not only to Havelock, but also to Dr Antonio Stalletti, who was well liked by him, and a frequent visitor to Selford Manor.

"Three weeks before Lord Selford's death, when he was suffering from an attack of delirium tremens, and in a very nervous state, Mr Havelock went to him and told him that he was on the verge of bankruptcy, that he had used some of his clients' money, including Lord Selford's, and asked his lordship if he would save him from a prosecution. The sum involved was not a very large one – £27,000; but Lord Selford was not the kind of man who would forgive such a breach of trust.

"He fell into a rage, threatening Havelock that he would institute a prosecution, and, as a result of his fury, he suffered a stroke and was carried to bed unconscious. Dr Stalletti was immediately called in, and, with the help of Elizabeth Cawler, the nurse of Lord Selford's young son, he recovered sufficiently to repeat, in the presence of Dr Stalletti, the accusation he had made against Havelock, the situation becoming further complicated by the fact that Silva, a Portuguese gardener, was in the room, having been called in with the idea of assisting the doctor to restrain his patient in his violence.

"Immediately afterwards, Lord Selford had a collapse, from which he did not recover, and he died on November 14th, there being present at his death Dr Stalletti, Mrs Cawler, and Havelock. The writer of this note did not appear till a much later period, and at the time was ignorant of the circumstances, but he hereby agrees that he was equally guilty with all the other signatories.

"Lord Selford had not time to change his will, by which he left Havelock his sole executor. It was Dr Stalletti (who by his signature attests) who suggested that nothing should be said about the circumstances attending his lordship's death, or about the statement he made just prior. To this Mr Havelock agreed (as he testifies by his signature) and a plan was formed whereby Havelock should administer the estate, the bulk of the revenues being divided equally between the four people who were privy to his lordship's accusation. The gardener, Silva, was then called in to the conference, and as he was a poor man and hated his lordship, who was a ready man with his cane if anything annoyed him, Silva agreed.

"It was at that time the intention of the four conspirators to enrich themselves to a moderate extent from the estate during the period of Mr Havelock's administration, and to leave it to Havelock, when the time came that he would be compelled to hand over his trust to the new Lord Selford, to straighten matters out. Young Lord Selford, however, was a boy of delicate constitution and weak intellect; and very little time elapsed before it became clear that an unexpected danger would confront the four. Mr Havelock pointed out that, if this boy was noticeably deficient, the Commissioners in Lunacy might be notified and appoint another trustee to administer the estate; and it was then decided to find a private school where the boy could be kept out of sight.

"The choice fell upon the writer, who had had the misfortune to be punished by the laws of the country for obtaining money by misrepresentation. I was approached by Mr Havelock soon after I came out of prison, and was told by him that he was guardian of a boy of weak intellect, who, it was necessary, should be tutored in a school which had no other scholars. A very handsome sum was offered to me, and I gladly accepted the post and the responsibility.

"He was brought to me in January, 1902, and I saw at once that any attempt to instil education into this unpromising receptacle was foredoomed to failure. I had many consultations with Mr Havelock and Dr Stalletti, who was also in bad odour with the authorities, and it was at one of these conferences that Dr Stalletti put forward his theory – namely, that, supposing he had a child in his care of sufficiently tender age, he could destroy its identity, not by any act of cruelty, but by suggestion or by some kind of hypnotism. Dr Stalletti's theory was that, if the vital forces are inhibited in one direction, they will find abnormal expression in another, and it was his desire to create what he called the perfect man, strong and obedient, having no will of his own, but subservient to the will of another. To this conclusion, he said, the biologists of the world were tending, and just as the bee delegated its reproductive functions to one queen bee, so the time would come when the world would be populated by unthinking workers, dominated by a number of select brains, reared and cultured for the purpose of exercising that authority. He promised that he would destroy the identity of the young Lord Selford so that, to all intents and purposes, he would cease to exist as a human unit, without actually endangering the life and safety of the conspirators, as would be the case if the child were made away with.

"I confess I was in favour of this scheme, but Mr Havelock was for a long time opposed, because, as he told us, he was not satisfied that the experiment would be a success. Dr Stalletti undertook, if he had a suitable subject, to prove it within three months; and after we had discussed the matter, Mrs Cawler said she would put at the doctor's disposal one of her two nephews. Mrs Cawler herself was childless, but she had the care of two children which had been put in her charge by her dead brother, who had also left a small sum for their maintenance. The child was transferred to Gallows Hill Cottage, and at the end of three months, though I did not see the result of the experiment, Mr Havelock told me that it had been successful and he had agreed to Selford leaving my care.

"I had already begun to draw on the revenues of the estate, but thinking that my position might be a precarious one if the boy was taken away from me, and if I had no actual proof that others shared my guilty knowledge, I asked that a legal agreement should be drawn up and filed in some place where we could all see it at the same time, but to which nobody else had access. I further asked that a statement in which we all admitted our share of responsibility should be kept in a similar place. There were long discussions about this. Stalletti was indifferent, Havelock was worried, and it was Mrs Cawler who suggested the plan which we eventually followed.

"I have told you that a tomb had been prepared for Lord Selford. It was that which had once been occupied by the founder of the house, and the door was ordered but was not in place when he died. He was, in point of fact, buried in Vault 6, the first on the left as you enter the tombs. Havelock immediately jumped at the idea. He had received the keys from the makers; the door had been hung; and there was, in the tomb itself, a place where such a document could be kept. We agreed eventually that it should take the shape which now appears.

"It was difficult to explain to Silva, who had a small knowledge of English but a great fund of low cunning, that we were not trying to incriminate him to save ourselves. But, fortunately, I had acquired in my student days a knowledge of the Portuguese language, and I was able, as will be seen herewith, to make a literal translation of this statement, which will be found on the final ten pages of the book and which has been signed by us all.

"At the moment of writing, Lord Selford is 'under tuition' at Gallows Hill, and from my own observation it seems that, both in the case of Mrs Cawler's nephew and in that of Lord Selford, the experiment has been highly successful. Already these boys come and go at the doctor's wish, make no complaint, and can endure even the rigours of a severe winter with the lightest clothes without any apparent discomfort. Since this first line was written, I have married Mrs Cawler, such an arrangement commending itself to Havelock and Stalletti…"

(The next few words were half obliterated by a savage black line that had been drawn through them, but Dick managed to decipher: "…although I had other plans for my future, I agreed.")

"It is extremely unlikely that our scheme will ever be detected. The Selfords are without relatives, the nearest heir to the property being a distant cousin; but he is a rich man and is unlikely to inquire too closely into the whereabouts of his lordship. Mr Havelock intends, when the boy reaches a maturer age, to announce that he has gone abroad on an extensive tour.

"To the truth of the foregoing we, the undersigned, set our hands."

Here followed the signatures, and on the next page began the Portuguese translation of the document.

33

"The letters that Havelock showed me," said Dick, as they were driving back to town, "were, of course, written by himself. I discovered that the day he showed me a message that he said he had received that morning from Cairo. It was written in green ink, and he had two specks of green ink on the tip of his finger. I knew before that that he was deeply involved in this case."

"How did Cawler know that the big man was his brother?" asked Sneed. "That puzzles me."

Dick thought the matter over.

"He may have guessed for a long time," he said. "He's not a bad fellow, Cawler, and I'm not going to repeat the story he told me about the scientific use of a spanner. At present the 'locals' think that it was caused by the car in its fall, and I see no reason in the world why I should undeceive them."

"Is your young lady's father a very rich man?" asked Sneed innocently, but quailed before Dick Martin's eye.

"Will you get it out of your head that Miss Sybil Lansdown is my 'young lady' in any respect whatever. Although her father was very rich at the time that document was written, he was a poor man when he died."

"The girl will be rich now, though," said Sneed.

"Yes," replied Dick shortly.

He had an uncomfortable feeling that the change in Sybil Lansdown's fortunes made a very considerable difference to him. He had enough money to be acquitted of any charge of fortune-hunting;

but, as he argued, a girl with the immense wealth of the Selfords at her command might well hesitate to limit the possibilities of her future by...

"Anyway, I haven't spoken a word to her about that," he said, unconsciously answering his own thoughts.

But Inspector Sneed was sleeping peacefully in a corner of the car and did not reply.

Dick went home and walked straight into his bedroom and pulled open the drawer of the bureau where, one grisly night, a silent figure had crouched.

"They've got him, Lew," he said quietly, and closed the door.

For, strange though it may sound, Dick's heart was hottest against Stalletti for this one crime.

He dressed himself with unusual care, rejecting this cravat and selecting that, changing his shoes twice, and went back, not once, but half a dozen times to his dressing-table, there to manipulate a hair brush with delicate care; and at last, feeling a little hot and uncomfortable, he took a cab and was deposited at the door of 107, Coram Street. Passing up the stairs, he pressed the bell of the apartment, and almost immediately it was opened by Sybil; and the look of relief in her face when she saw him was a great reward.

"Thank God, you're safe," she said in a low voice. "I know that something dreadful has happened. I've only seen what was in the early editions. Mr Havelock is arrested – how terrible!"

He nodded.

"Mother isn't here," she said, and dropped her eyes. "She thought – she thought – perhaps – you would come, and that you'd like – " She did not finish her sentence.

"And that I should like to see you alone? I think I should, Sybil," he said quietly. "Do you know you're a very rich woman?"

She looked at him incredulously.

"Lord Selford is dead. You are the heiress-at-law," he stated briefly, and then: "Is it going to make a big difference?"

"How?" she asked.

"I mean" – he was almost tongue-tied – "is it going to make you think any differently in – the way you think of me?"

"How do I think of you now?" she asked, with a return to her old manner.

He pushed his fingers through his finely brushed hair.

"I don't know," he admitted lamely. And then a bright idea occurred to him. "Would you like me to tell you what I think of *you*?"

For answer she took him by the arm, led him into the sitting-room and, closing the door, pushed him gently into a chair.

"I should, very much," she breathed, and sat on the arm of the chair expectantly.

Edgar Wallace

Big Foot

Footprints and a dead woman bring together Superintendent Minton and the amateur sleuth Mr Cardew. Who is the man in the shrubbery? Who is the singer of the haunting Moorish tune? Why is Hannah Shaw so determined to go to Pawsy, 'a dog lonely place' she had previously detested? Death lurks in the dark and someone must solve the mystery before BIG FOOT strikes again, in a yet more fiendish manner.

Bones In London

The new Managing Director of Schemes Ltd has an elegant London office and a theatrically dressed assistant – however Bones, as he is better known, is bored. Luckily there is a slump in the shipping market and it is not long before Joe and Fred Pole pay Bones a visit. They are totally unprepared for Bones' unnerving style of doing business, unprepared for his unique style of innocent and endearing mischief.

Edgar Wallace

Bones of the River

'Taking the little paper from the pigeon's leg, Hamilton saw it was from Sanders and marked URGENT. *Send Bones instantly to Lujamalababa... Arrest and bring to head-quarters the witch doctor.*'

It is a time when the world's most powerful nations are vying for colonial honour, a time of trading steamers and tribal chiefs. In the mysterious African territories administered by Commissioner Sanders, Bones persistently manages to create his own unique style of innocent and endearing mischief.

The Daffodil Mystery

When Mr Thomas Lyne, poet, poseur and owner of Lyne's Emporium insults a cashier, Odette Rider, she resigns. Having summoned detective Jack Tarling to investigate another employee, Mr Milburgh, Lyne now changes his plans. Tarling and his Chinese companion refuse to become involved. They pay a visit to Odette's flat. In the hall Tarling meets Sam, convicted felon and protégé of Lyne. Next morning Tarling discovers a body. The hands are crossed on the breast, adorned with a handful of daffodils.

Edgar Wallace

The Joker

While the millionaire Stratford Harlow is in Princetown, not only does he meet with his lawyer Mr Ellenbury but he gets his first glimpse of the beautiful Aileen Rivers, niece of the actor and convicted felon Arthur Ingle. When Aileen is involved in a car accident on the Thames Embankment, the driver is James Carlton of Scotland Yard. Later that evening Carlton gets a call. It is Aileen. She needs help.

The Square Emerald
(USA: The Girl from Scotland Yard)

'Suicide on the left,' says Chief Inspector Coldwell pleasantly, as he and Leslie Maughan stride along the Thames Embankment during a brutally cold night. A gaunt figure is sprawled across the parapet. But Coldwell soon discovers that Peter Dawlish, fresh out of prison for forgery, is not considering suicide but murder. Coldwell suspects Druze as the intended victim. Maughan disagrees. If Druze dies, she says, 'It will be because he does not love children!'

OTHER TITLES BY EDGAR WALLACE AVAILABLE DIRECT FROM HOUSE OF STRATUS

Quantity		£	$(US)	$(CAN)	€
☐	THE ADMIRABLE CARFEW	6.99	12.95	19.95	13.50
☐	THE ANGEL OF TERROR	6.99	12.95	19.95	13.50
☐	THE AVENGER (USA: THE HAIRY ARM)	6.99	12.95	19.95	13.50
☐	BARBARA ON HER OWN	6.99	12.95	19.95	13.50
☐	BIG FOOT	6.99	12.95	19.95	13.50
☐	THE BLACK ABBOT	6.99	12.95	19.95	13.50
☐	BONES	6.99	12.95	19.95	13.50
☐	BONES IN LONDON	6.99	12.95	19.95	13.50
☐	BONES OF THE RIVER	6.99	12.95	19.95	13.50
☐	THE CLUE OF THE NEW PIN	6.99	12.95	19.95	13.50
☐	THE CLUE OF THE SILVER KEY	6.99	12.95	19.95	13.50
☐	THE CLUE OF THE TWISTED CANDLE	6.99	12.95	19.95	13.50
☐	THE COAT OF ARMS (USA: THE ARRANWAYS MYSTERY)	6.99	12.95	19.95	13.50
☐	THE COUNCIL OF JUSTICE	6.99	12.95	19.95	13.50
☐	THE CRIMSON CIRCLE	6.99	12.95	19.95	13.50
☐	THE DAFFODIL MYSTERY	6.99	12.95	19.95	13.50
☐	THE DARK EYES OF LONDON (USA: THE CROAKERS)	6.99	12.95	19.95	13.50
☐	THE DAUGHTERS OF THE NIGHT	6.99	12.95	19.95	13.50
☐	A DEBT DISCHARGED	6.99	12.95	19.95	13.50
☐	THE DEVIL MAN	6.99	12.95	19.95	13.50
☐	THE DUKE IN THE SUBURBS	6.99	12.95	19.95	13.50
☐	THE FACE IN THE NIGHT	6.99	12.95	19.95	13.50
☐	THE FEATHERED SERPENT	6.99	12.95	19.95	13.50
☐	THE FLYING SQUAD	6.99	12.95	19.95	13.50
☐	THE FORGER (USA: THE CLEVER ONE)	6.99	12.95	19.95	13.50
☐	THE FOUR JUST MEN	6.99	12.95	19.95	13.50
☐	FOUR SQUARE JANE	6.99	12.95	19.95	13.50
☐	THE FOURTH PLAGUE	6.99	12.95	19.95	13.50

ALL HOUSE OF STRATUS BOOKS ARE AVAILABLE FROM GOOD BOOKSHOPS OR DIRECT FROM THE PUBLISHER:

Internet: www.houseofstratus.com including author interviews, reviews, features.

Email: sales@houseofstratus.com please quote author, title and credit card details.

OTHER TITLES BY EDGAR WALLACE AVAILABLE DIRECT FROM HOUSE OF STRATUS

Quantity		£	$(US)	$(CAN)	€
☐	THE FRIGHTENED LADY	6.99	12.95	19.95	13.50
☐	GOOD EVANS	6.99	12.95	19.95	13.50
☐	THE HAND OF POWER	6.99	12.95	19.95	13.50
☐	THE IRON GRIP	6.99	12.95	19.95	13.50
☐	THE JOKER (USA: THE COLOSSUS)	6.99	12.95	19.95	13.50
☐	THE JUST MEN OF CORDOVA	6.99	12.95	19.95	13.50
☐	THE KEEPERS OF THE KING'S PEACE	6.99	12.95	19.95	13.50
☐	THE LAW OF THE FOUR JUST MEN	6.99	12.95	19.95	13.50
☐	THE LONE HOUSE MYSTERY	6.99	12.95	19.95	13.50
☐	THE MAN WHO BOUGHT LONDON	6.99	12.95	19.95	13.50
☐	THE MAN WHO KNEW	6.99	12.95	19.95	13.50
☐	THE MAN WHO WAS NOBODY	6.99	12.95	19.95	13.50
☐	THE MIND OF MR J G REEDER (USA: THE MURDER BOOK OF J G REEDER)	6.99	12.95	19.95	13.50
☐	MORE EDUCATED EVANS	6.99	12.95	19.95	13.50
☐	MR J G REEDER RETURNS (USA: MR REEDER RETURNS)	6.99	12.95	19.95	13.50
☐	MR JUSTICE MAXELL	6.99	12.95	19.95	13.50
☐	RED ACES	6.99	12.95	19.95	13.50
☐	ROOM 13	6.99	12.95	19.95	13.50
☐	SANDERS	6.99	12.95	19.95	13.50
☐	SANDERS OF THE RIVER	6.99	12.95	19.95	13.50
☐	THE SINISTER MAN	6.99	12.95	19.95	13.50
☐	THE SQUARE EMERALD (USA: THE GIRL FROM SCOTLAND YARD)	6.99	12.95	19.95	13.50
☐	THE THREE JUST MEN	6.99	12.95	19.95	13.50
☐	THE THREE OAK MYSTERY	6.99	12.95	19.95	13.50
☐	THE TRAITOR'S GATE	6.99	12.95	19.95	13.50
☐	WHEN THE GANGS CAME TO LONDON	6.99	12.95	19.95	13.50

Order Line: UK: 0800 169 1780,
USA: 1 800 509 9942
INTERNATIONAL: +44 (0) 20 7494 6400 (UK)
or +01 212 218 7649
(please quote author, title, and credit card details.)

Send to: House of Stratus Sales Department
24c Old Burlington Street
London
W1X 1RL
UK

House of Stratus Inc.
Suite 210
1270 Avenue of the Americas
New York • NY 10020
USA

PAYMENT

Please tick currency you wish to use:

☐ £ (Sterling)   ☐ $ (US)   ☐ $ (CAN)   ☐ € (Euros)

Allow for shipping costs charged per order plus an amount per book as set out in the tables below:

CURRENCY/DESTINATION

	£(Sterling)	$(US)	$(CAN)	€(Euros)
Cost per order				
UK	1.50	2.25	3.50	2.50
Europe	3.00	4.50	6.75	5.00
North America	3.00	3.50	5.25	5.00
Rest of World	3.00	4.50	6.75	5.00
Additional cost per book				
UK	0.50	0.75	1.15	0.85
Europe	1.00	1.50	2.25	1.70
North America	1.00	1.00	1.50	1.70
Rest of World	1.50	2.25	3.50	3.00

PLEASE SEND CHEQUE OR INTERNATIONAL MONEY ORDER.
payable to: STRATUS HOLDINGS plc or HOUSE OF STRATUS INC. or card payment as indicated

STERLING EXAMPLE

Cost of book(s):...................... Example: 3 x books at £6.99 each: £20.97
Cost of order: .... Example: £1.50 (Delivery to UK address)
Additional cost per book:.............. Example: 3 x £0.50: £1.50
Order total including shipping:.......... Example: £23.97

VISA, MASTERCARD, SWITCH, AMEX:

☐☐☐☐ ☐☐☐☐ ☐☐☐☐ ☐☐☐☐ ☐☐☐☐

Issue number (Switch only):
☐☐☐

Start Date: **Expiry Date:**
☐☐/☐☐   ☐☐/☐☐

Signature: _____

NAME: _____

ADDRESS: _____

COUNTRY: _____

ZIP/POSTCODE: _____

Please allow 28 days for delivery. Despatch normally within 48 hours.

Prices subject to change without notice.
Please tick box if you do not wish to receive any additional information. ☐

House of Stratus publishes many other titles in this genre; please check our website (**www.houseofstratus.com**) for more details.